Where It Begins

by Leigha Jaclynn

DORRANCE
PUBLISHING CO
EST. 1920
PITTSBURGH, PENNSYLVANIA 15238

Dorrance Publishing Co
585 Alpha Drive
Pittsburgh, PA 15238
Visit our website at *www.dorrancebookstore.com*

ISBN: 978-1-4809-8261-1
eISBN: 978-1-4809-8237-6

Chapter One

Carter

I opened my eyes and looked around the room. It was new, but the furniture was all the same. Large windows lined the off-white walls, all of them letting in the early morning sun. I rubbed my eyes and sighed. I needed to go get curtains, immediately. I pulled the comforter aside and got up slowly, stretching my sore body. I had spent the whole weekend unpacking from the move—I hated the idea of not being settled. I picked up the small cluster of pills resting in the tiny ceramic dish besides my bed and washed them down with the glass of water from the night before. I got up and walked over to my closet, opening the folding double doors.

"Come on, Carter, I can't be late for my first day," Dani, my little sister, said opening my bedroom door. No knock, per usual.

"I'm looking for something to wear, give me a break." I grabbed a black bra, hooking it over my tank top before pulling it off.

"Well, come on," she groaned, impatient as ever. I pulled on a pair of dark blue skinny jeans and my well-worn black lace up boots. "Here, just wear this." she tossed me a soft, grey t-shirt that was hanging off the back of my desk chair. I shrugged, pulling it on, then grabbed my beat-up leather bomber jacket.

"God, why can't you dress like a girl?" she groaned, examining herself in my mirror. I looked her up and down; she was wearing a pink sundress and gladiator sandals, her blonde hair in long curls—a look that probably took at least an hour to achieve, requiring her to get up before the sun even rose, I could only assume. I smiled to myself and pulled my hair out of its loose bun atop my head and shook it out. My look took under 10 minutes and I was able to get as much sleep as I possibly could.

"Why are you so excited for school? It's already half way through the first semester, and you're only a sophomore," I chuckled softly at the last part. I ran some oil through my dry, knotty hair and watched her pick invisible lint from her pristine dress behind me in the mirror.

"Because I get to start over, no more stupid little Danielle from Oregon. I'm now cool, soon to be popular Dani in Massachusetts who doesn't have a sister with anger issues," she said, emphasizing the last part before skipping out. I picked up a sneaker that was lying haphazardly on the floor by my desk and threw it through the door. She let out an unnecessary scream and called out to Dad.

"Dad! She threw a shoe at me!" Her shrill voice echoed through the empty house.

"Dad left two hours ago," I called after her, grabbing my bag. I gave myself one last look in the mirror then grabbed my keys off my desk.

As I tromped down the stairs from my room to the garage, I saw Dani already waiting by my old blue pick-up truck, applying another coat of lip stick in the side mirror. I smirked to myself and unlocked the doors, climbing in. Dani tucked her lipstick into her backpack and got in, slamming the door closed. I jumped at the sudden noise and looked at her, eyes wide.

"What the hell, Dani?"

"I'm honestly surprised this hunk of crap made it all the way across the country," she said, looking at the dated interior, obviously ignoring my annoyed stare.

"If you want rides to school don't go calling my truck a hunk of crap," I shot back. She threw her hands up in mock defense then looked out the window. I drove us to our new school in silence, parked, and as I tried to get out my door got stuck. I pushed on the door, nothing, then pulled the handle again, still nothing. I felt my cheeks grow hot and I slammed the full force of my shoulder and side against the door. It didn't budge.

"Bye!" Dani laughed, getting out with ease. Everything came to her with ease. I groaned and leaned back, kicking the door with both feet—whether it was out of anger or in hopes of helping dislodge it, I wasn't sure. What happened next knocked the wind right out of me. Unsure if my repeated hitting of the door was a little too hard or if the truck is a little too old, but the door flung off. It hit a guy riding by on a motorcycle and he stopped short, jumping off.

"What the fuck?!" he yelled, ripping his helmet off his head and throwing it on the ground. He turned and looked at me and his mouth fell open slightly, then he snapped it shut, regaining his composure—and anger—very quickly.

"Don't yell at me," I yelled back, finally able to breathe again. I jumped out of the opening on my

5

side of the cab, grabbed my door with all my might, and heaved it into the truck bed. He watched in awe, his jaw slack, as I grabbed my bag and keys and walked off.

"You seriously need to work on those anger issues," Dani said as I walked away, somehow appearing from nowhere and falling into my fast pace trek towards the school.

"He was hot, probably has anger issues too, I'm guessing. Perfect for you, you can go to meetings together!" she said fake-excitedly, laughing at her own dumb joke.

"Funny. Don't make me hurt you," I snapped, seething.

"Bye," she squealed, running away. I stomped off and headed to class, my cheeks still hot with anger.

Walking into my first class, I was still fuming from what had just happened. I saw an empty seat in the back of the second to last row by the windows and took it, hoping the teacher wouldn't even notice my presence. The classroom was nearly full when the bell rang and the teacher, an elderly man, balding and pudgy, pushed himself away from his desk to get up and close the door. Right as he was pulling it closed, an arm shot through the crack and the man groaned, opening the door just wide enough for the person to slide in sideways, their back to the classroom. It was him—the guy from the motorcycle. I slumped in my seat, hoping to make myself as small as possible. I did not need his attitude or attention right now.

"Mr. Hastings, thank you for gracing us with your presence. Please find a seat, you have already robbed your fellow students of enough class time," the teacher said, his voice low and clipped. "Hastings" looked at the class, then his eyes narrowed on me. His wide lips twisted into a smirk and he walked down my row and stared at the kid in the seat behind me. After a few seconds, the kid grabbed his stuff and scrambled to an empty desk in the front. The guy slid into the seat directly be-hind me, putting his backpack on his desk. I kept my eyes trained on the board, body faced forward. I heard the chair squeak as he moved, then I could feel his body heat as he leaned in close to my ear.

"You're in my seat, new girl." He whispered. Chills ran down my spine. I straightened my pos-ture and kept my eyes forward. His voice was smooth and low, with perfect cadence. It was al-most too eloquent, not at all what I expected. I needed to stop thinking about him. I needed to think of a comeback. I looked at the desk, etched into it in pen were some faded doodles, some curse words, and "Mr. Eaton sucks ass" in a chicken scratch scrawl.

"I don't see your name on it," I replied, my fingers curling around the edge of the plastic desktop. He let out a small chuckle. The hairs on my neck all rose—from anger or exhilaration I wasn't sure.

"Honey, you don't even know my name," he said in my ear again, his breath hot against my skin.

The second he let that pet name slip, I knew I felt the former.

"Unless it's Mr. Eaton sucks ass, which I highly doubt it is, I don't want or need to know your name," I scoffed, my blood running hot. He let out a laugh and the teacher turned, a scowl on his pale face as his beady eyes narrowed in on "Hastings".

"Excuse me, Mr. Hastings, and…who are you, again?" The teacher said, walking over to our desks, he barely gave me a second glance, his eyes were focused on the boy behind me.

"Carter Baker, sir, I just started here today," I said, my shoulders tense, fingernails scraping against the underside of the desk as I gripped it harder.

"Well, Ms. Baker, I suggest you find a different student to help welcome you to our fine scholastic institution," he said, giving "Hastings" behind me a terse look. Some of the students snickered behind the teacher and I could hear him lean back in his chair.

"I don't know, Mr. Eaton, she might be a troublemaker, she just said that you suck ass, so…" he trailed off. I whipped around in my seat to give him my dirtiest look. He had a wry smile on his face and his eyes were alight. This was all a big joke to him.

"Screw you, asshole," I shot back, and his eyes widened, a hint of surprise crossed his face. A couple students gasped and started to whisper.

"That's enough!" Mr. Eaton snapped, "Mr. Hastings, please do us all a favor and escort yourself down to the principal's office," he said, his voice stern. Hastings got up and slung his backpack over his shoulder and walked out, a smile on his face.

"And as for you, Ms. Baker, I hope outbursts like that won't be a common occurrence this year. As you can tell, I have a very short tolerance for tomfoolery," he stated before turning on his heel and making his way down the row of desks. I sunk down even further in my seat, reeling with anger. Off to a great fresh start. I just hoped that kid wasn't in any of my other classes.

At lunch, I got a salad and wandered through the raucous cafeteria till I saw a door that led outside. It was a small courtyard lined with a short brick fence, a few small picnic tables scattered around the center. I sat on the brick wall, my legs dangling on either side, food in front of me.

The guy from earlier, Hastings, walked outside and looked around. I hadn't really had a chance to look at him—really look at him—and I took a minute to check him out before he spotted me. He was tall and broad shouldered, with tousled jet-black hair, pale olive skin, dark green eyes, pink lips, and bone structure to die for. He was wearing scuffed up jeans, a white Henley t-shirt, and beat up black leather jacket.

He saw me and walked over, a coy smile on his wide lips.

"You know, you're lucky you didn't mess up my bike," he said, putting one hand on the pillar I was leaning against, the other by my thighs, effectively boxing me in.

"Why, what would you do about it?" I replied, sarcasm dripping off every word.

"You don't want to know," he grinned and took a cigarette out of a pack in his jacket pocket.

"Don't think about lighting that in my face," I breathed. I could feel my cheeks flush.

"Why, what are *you* going to do about it?" he retorted, mocking me as he popped a silver lighter open, his thumb on the spark. Plucking the cigarette out of his mouth, I ripped it in half then tossed it on the ground. He smiled and popped another in his mouth. Clearly, he just enjoyed messing with me.

"Move." I pushed him so I could get down. He didn't budge. I could feel the rage begin to surface in me.

"Aw come on, baby, don't be like that," he joked, closing me in more within his long, muscular arms. Again, with the pet names. My cheeks burned, and my breathing grew shallow.

"Don't call me baby," I said before shoving him harder, grabbing my bag, and walking away.

"Bye, baby," he called after me. I stopped, my nails digging into the palms of my hands. I took deep breaths like my old anger management coach had tried to teach me. That was, before I punched him in our first session.

Chapter Two

Carter

At the end of the day Dani was leaning against my truck when I walked over. I tossed my backpack into the hole where my door used to be and swiped some fallen leaves off the bench seat. Dani climbed in and placed her bag by her feet then crossed her legs, smoothing the hem of her dress over her thighs.

"I need to go to the school auto shop garage before it closes to get the door fixed," I said as I climbed in. I instinctively went to pull my door closed but it wasn't there. I cursed under my breath, shoved my key into the ignition and drove down to the garage.

"Stay in the truck," I warned, getting out. She pouted like a child and crossed her arms in an act of defiance. I groaned. She could be so petulant at times.

"Hey, is anyone here?" I called, walking through the open garage door of the shop. Loud, screeching metal music was blasting from a radio. I kicked it off and slammed my hand down on the hood of a car. "Hello!" I shouted.

"Hey!" someone yelled angrily. They rolled out from under the car I had just smacked and it was him, Hastings, shirtless and covered in oil and grease. I couldn't help but look at his bare torso, where a large, lilac colored bruise was forming on his right arm and side, presumably from where my door had hit him.

"Dear God, what are you doing here?" he groaned, standing and wiping off his very chiseled chest with a rag from his back pocket. "What do you want? You're not stalking me, are you?" He smiled, his eyebrows arched. I took a deep breath and scuffed my boot into the cement floor.

"I want my door re-attached to my car, duh," I said, pointing to my truck where Dani was now leaning against the passenger side. I groaned, this day was just getting worse and worse.

"Who's she?" he asked, nodding his chin towards Dani. She was leaning against the hood and curling a long piece of blond hair around her finger.

"My little sister, she's fifteen," I crossed my arms. He smiled and waved at her. She giggled and did her flirty finger wave back. "Fifteen, dumbass, now where's someone who can help me fix my door?"

"I can," a guy said, running out. He had a blond buzz cut, bright blue eyes, and a baby face. He was wearing a pair of grey joggers and a faded maroon shirt with the school logo and "wrestling team" printed on it. He stood next to Hastings, who laughed at him.

"Kent, you're not in auto class," he rolled his eyes at the boy.

"But she's hot," he smiled at me, giving me a wink. I wanted to vomit.

"I'd like someone who knows what they're doing, thank you very much," I smiled a tight smile, pushing him away with a finger.

"Aw come on, baby," he smiled at me, his eyes running up and down my body. What was with the boys at this school and pet names? I bunched my fists and crossed my arms.

"Don't go there, Kent, she kicked that door off her truck today. Oh, and she got me a week's worth of detention," Hastings smiled, nudging Kent with his elbow.

"Shit," he laughed, "Why don't you help her, Jag?" he chided, patting "Jag" on the shoulder.

"I rather not, if I don't fix it perfectly she might attack me," he said with a smirk on his smug face. I dug my nails into my palms and breathed in and out, my fists were still stuffed under my crossed arms.

"Forget it, I'll go somewhere else," I sighed, giving up and turning towards my truck.

"Stop harassing the poor girl," another guy said walking out, this one older and in blue coveralls.

"Can you help me fix my door?" I asked, slightly desperate to just get the job done and get out of this place. He nodded and smiled at me. I jogged out to where I had parked the truck outside and Dani was back in the cab now.

"Are we leaving? I'm bored," she pouted. I laughed at her and motioned to the bench a few yards away.

"I'm getting my door fixed, wait there," I said, turning the engine on.

"You're joking, right?" She scoffed, jaw slightly ajar. I stared at her with a look I hoped conveyed my lack of humor and after a few seconds she groaned, grabbed her bag, and got out of the cab. I smiled and pulled into an open bay of the garage. I was talking to the third guy, who happened to be the shop class teacher, when I heard Kent say something to Jag. I glanced over and saw Dani walking over.

"Can we go home any time this century?" She said, walking past Kent and Jag, flashing them a smile before zeroing in on me.

"Who is that?" Kent smiled a greasy smile, whistling at the sight of her.

"My fifteen-year-old sister," I snapped back.

"Relax, girlfriend," he said, putting his hands up in defense, probably thinking about what Jag had said earlier about me attacking him.

"Breath, Carter, we don't need another episode," Dani groaned, flipping her hair dramatically. I gave her a death glare, then glanced at Jag. His eyebrows were raised and I could tell he heard exactly what she had said, and was processing this new information carefully. I shoved her and pointed towards the open garage door.

"Outside, come on. We're going to wait on the bench, just let me know when it's done," I said, dragging her outside with me.

About forty-five excruciatingly slow minutes later, the teacher, Mr. Wexler, came out of the garage and walked over.

"Door's all fixed," Mr. Wexler said, wiping his hands on a rag.

"Thanks," I smiled, "Come on, Dani, let's go."

"Finally," she groaned, getting in the cab. I climbed in and closed the door, then rolled down the window as he walked over.

"It shouldn't get stuck anymore, and if it does, don't kick it again," he smiled, patting the window sill. I smiled and nodded, thanking him as the engine turned over.

"Bye, boys," Dani waved, leaning out the window, giving them a healthy view of her budding cleavage. They shoved each other and Kent waved back.

"You're fifteen, give it a break," I said, pulling out of the garage and driving towards home.

"It's fine," she laughed, waving me off.

"No, it's not," I sighed, gripping the steering

wheel. She flipped her hair and looked out the window.

"Jag is hot," she said after some silence.

"What kind of name is Jag?" I said, mostly to myself.

"He has a banging body," she went on, clearly not listening to me.

"And who doesn't wear a shirt when working on a car?!" I rambled.

"Hot people, and I think he likes you," she finished. I stopped short at a red light and looked at her.

"Breathe," she said, eyes wide.

"I really hate you," I groaned, speeding the rest of the way home.

"Whatever," she looked out the window, her arms crossed again.

When we got home I grabbed my bag and went inside. Dani went upstairs and I went to my bedroom, a converted loft over the garage. I opened the door and put my bag on my desk, already cluttered with photographs I had yet to hang up. I kicked off my shoes and fell back on my bed.

"What kind of name is Jag?" I said out loud to myself, laughing as I ran my fingers through my hair.

Chapter Three

Jagger

It was a week since Carter had moved into town and completely turned my world upside down. I couldn't wait to go to school now, U. S. History with Mr. Eaton had officially made its way from my least favorite class to my favorite class, and that was saying a lot. I sat in the last seat of the row, waiting for Carter to walk in. I tried not to look so obvious, watching the door out of my peripherals.

Finally, she breezed in, head down as she walked past Eaton, who, as always, was wedged behind his small desk. She turned down the row and her eyes darted at me then back down on the ground. Her long brown hair was tied in a loose knot, strands falling around her make-up free face. She was wearing a loose, maroon long sleeve shirt over black leggings and a pair of knee high boots. She dropped her bag on the floor and slid into the chair.

"Morning, sunshine," I said. She groaned, sitting up straight. "What's wrong, sweetheart, wake up on the wrong side of the bed?" I mused. She scoffed. "You know what's a good fix for that?" I said, leaning over the desk, getting close to her.

"You are such a pig," she groaned, giving me a dirty look over her shoulder. I blew her a kiss and she scoffed.

"Alright class, let's begin," Mr. Eaton said, walking back from closing the door after the bell rang. He glanced at my seat, with me in it, and raised his bushy white eyebrows.

"Mr. Hastings, what an honor it is for you to be with us today, and before the bell too." He smirked, before turning to the board.

"I heard somewhere that he sucks ass," I whispered in her ear. She shoved her shoulder at me, shaking me off as if I was a fly buzzing around her, and I smiled and sat back, crossing my arms. After class, she grabbed her bag and I fell into step with her.

"Where you off to now?" I asked, shouldering my bag.

"Class, what's it to you?" she said, eyes trained forward.

"Ooh, me too, it's like were at school or something," I smirked. She imitated me, mocked what I said under her breath and I smiled.

"Girls got some spunk to her, I like it," I smiled, and out of the corner of my eye I saw a small blush come across her cheeks. I smiled, I couldn't help it. There was something about her that drew me to her, like a moth to a flame. I knew I was playing with fire, but I liked it.

"So, what is this, now you're the one stalking me?" she said, throwing my own words back in my face. I stopped in my tracks and she kept walking then turned.

"What? Can't stand the heat then get out of the kitchen, Hastings," she smirked, walking backwards before turning on her heel. I smiled and jogged to catch up.

Slowly over the next couple of weeks, I couldn't help but ease up on her. Sure, she had hit me with her car door and had been a nuisance in the beginning. But she was beautiful, funny, smart, and could not only take it but dish it right back. Sitting in U. S. History, waiting for her to walk in had become the best part of my day. She walked in, her long, chestnut hair in two French braids, a white hoodie under her beat up old leather jacket and faded blue jeans. She never wore much make-up, she didn't even need it, anyways. She had big brown eyes, the cutest button nose, and lips that screamed "kiss me." She slid into the seat in front of me and I smiled. I tugged on the end of her braid and she looked at me over her shoulder.

"What is this, kindergarten?" she said under her breath. I smiled and leaned over my desk.

"Just wait until recess, I plan on knocking you down on the playground," I whispered in her ear. She laughed and then covered her mouth, stifling it. Eaton turned to look at us.

"Ah, yes, Mr. Hastings, care to put in your two cents?" he said, his hands on his wide hips.

"Uh yeah, the Emancipation Proclamation, total bullshit," I quipped.

A couple students snickered and Carter giggled again, her hand still over her mouth.

"Excuse me, Mr. Hastings? We're discussing Pearl Harbor," Eaton said, shortly taken aback before regaining his composure.

"Oh, that? Yeah, total bullshit, too," I said, tapping my pen on my desk.

Carter burst out laughing and Eaton's face turned beet red.

"Detention, both of you!" he fumed before turning back to the board. I twirled the end of Carter's braid around my finger.

"Sounds like a date," I whispered in her ear before tugging on the brown tresses.

After the final bell rang, I went to the study hall room where detention was held. Kent was sitting in the second row, Carter in the back, and a few other regulars were scattered around the room. Kent held up a closed fist as I walked past and I smiled and bumped mine to his then shoved him and went to sit next to Carter.

"The Emancipation Proclamation is total bullshit?" she stated, a coy smile on her lips. We laughed and I ran my fingers through my hair. I smiled and shrugged, man how I loved her laugh.

I sighed and sat back, looking at her. She had taken off her sweatshirt and was wearing a light blue t-shirt with a large, faded anchor on it. I recognized the logo, it was an underground rock band that split up before they could release a second album—and their first was nearly impossible to find anymore.

"You know the Anchors?" I asked, still in disbelief. She laughed and looked at me.

"*You* know them?" she said, same amount of disbelief on her face. I nodded.

"I saw them live in the city, one of their first shows," I said. She groaned, a small smile on her lips, eyes flashing with what I could only guess was envy.

"I am so jealous, I had tickets to their tour but they broke up," she said, "And I can't even find a copy of their first album that doesn't cost a fortune." She sighed, crossing her legs and leaning on her desk towards me. I smiled, an idea coming to mind. I was about to say something to her when the door slammed shut.

"Alright students, detention is for homework or silent reflection on why you are here," Mr. Copeland, the gym teacher, said, walking in. Carter sighed and sat straight forward and I followed suit.

Throughout the hour I stole glances at Carter, she was diligently doing her homework. I smiled and sat back, my hands behind my head, fingers intertwined, and leaned back, letting out a long, loud yawn as I stretched back. Mr. Copeland looked up over his 'Health and Fitness' magazine. I saw Carter look at me then back at her work. I scooted the chair back, making a loud scraping noise, and extended my legs, putting my feet on my desk, and crossed them. Carter stifled a giggle and Mr. Copeland sat back, putting his magazine down.

"Excuse me, Mr. Hastings, but this isn't your home. Please put your feet down and do some homework," he said dryly.

"But Mr. Copeland, you said we could reflect silently on why we were here, I was just doing that," I said with a mock innocence. Carter chuckled and looked down. Kent let out a laugh. Mr. Copeland looked at Kent, who shut up immediately—Copeland was also the wrestling team's coach and could make or break Kent. He shifted his gaze to Carter, who kept her face down. He gave me a look of pure distain and picked up his magazine again. I looked at Carter, waggling my eyebrows and she smiled, shaking her head slowly.

That night I went home and rummaged through some drawers until I found the tape. It was the band's first and only album. I turned it over and over in my hands, one side was stamped with their logo, the other side had "Sinking" written in black sharpie—the name of the album. I smiled, tapping it against my palm, thinking about how I should go about my plan. Then, the idea hit me, I smiled to myself and looked through some more drawers until I found a small manila envelope and a sharpie. I wrote down my favorite lyric—"I was sinking until you pulled me up, you rescued me"—and slipped the tape into the envelope. I went to bed with a smile on my face, thinking of Carter and how excited she would be.

The next day after school I left the envelope with the tape on the hood of her truck and watched from afar. I saw her and Dani walk to the truck and Carter picked up the envelope, read the front, a smile growing on her lips before she opened it, looked at it, then immediately started to look around. She didn't see me, and she looked down, smiling to herself. Her smile was beautiful, infectious even, I couldn't help but grin at the sight of it. Still smiling I got on my bike, and watched her drive off, the first song on the album pumping through the open windows of her truck. I smiled and pulled my helmet on and revved my engine, heading down to the auto shop.

After a couple hours working in the garage, I left and headed over to my bike, which was parked in the lot adjacent to the field house. I saw Kent and some other guys from the wrestling team standing outside the entrance to the large field house, they must have just gotten out of practice. Kent noticed me, said something to the guys, and jogged over.

"What's up, man?" he said, flipping his keys up in the air. I snatched them before he could catch them and he chuckled. "What's got you in this chipper mood you've been in lately?" he smiled, catching the keys as I tossed them to him. I shrugged and lit a cigarette, and he smiled at me. "Does it have anything to do with that new girl?" He nudged me and I shrugged, taking a long drag.

"She's cool," I said, trying to play it off, but once he called me out on it, I realized that she was the reason I had been in a better mood lately.

"Don't get all soft on me now," He laughed, shouldering his gym bag, and I laughed, shoving him. He smiled his trademark dumb grin and we laughed. I finished my cigarette, dropping it on the pavement before stomping it with my boot.

"She does seem pretty cool," he said, nodding slowly. I shrugged and looked around, trying not to look at him. I knew if I did he would push further.

"Hot, too," he added. I smirked and looked down at my scuffed-up boots.

"She is beautiful," I agreed, and I saw him look at me, his blue eyes wide.

"Damn, do you like this girl?" he asked, slightly shocked.

"Shut up, Kent," I laughed, sitting down on my bike. He looked at me, his hands in the pockets of his sweatpants, a coy smile on his face.

"Jagger loves Carter," he sang, and I smacked him in the gut with the back of my hand. He doubled over and I laughed.

"You're an idiot, dude," I said, pulling my helmet on. I drove off, and when I looked in my side mirror I saw him watching me ride off. I flipped him off and he did the same. I smiled and turned the corner, heading home.

As I drove I thought about Carter, and what Kent said. He might be an idiot, but he was an astute one about this. I did like her, but I needed to figure out how to go about this. Especially with Kent and his blabber mouth. I pushed the thoughts aside and rode home, trying not to think about her smile.

Chapter Four

Carter

I was lying in bed reading when Dani waltzed in, ignoring the warning of my previously closed door. She was wearing a skin-tight black strapless dress that barely went down to her mid-thigh and wedges. She looked like a wanna-be Barbie playing dress up. Then I noticed the thin black whiskers drawn on her rosy cheeks and pink circle on her nose. She was clutching a pair of cat ears, and I remembered it was Halloween on Tuesday.

"Drive me to West's party," she said, glossing up her already overly glossed lips in my mirror.

"No, get out of my room," I threw a pillow at her.

"I'll tell Dad you're not a virgin if you don't," she sang as she continued to examine her face in my mirror.

I groaned and put my book down over my face. "I will forever regret telling you that," I grumbled into the pages of my book. She giggled and I sighed. I got up and grabbed my Converses. I was wearing rolled up boxer shorts and a tank top so I grabbed my leather jacket and pulled it on as we walked down the staircase from my room to the garage. We got in my truck and I drove to the address she gave me and parked outside.

"How are you going to get home?" I asked as she rummaged through her microscopic purse.

"You, obviously," she said as if I were stupid for even asking the question.

"What, no!" I laughed at her ignorance.

"Please, Car?" she begged, puppy dog eyes and all.

"You have one hour, go," I groaned. She clapped and squealed, then ran out and into a group of girls who all hugged her. I sighed and sat back and opened the glove box, taking out a book I kept there, opening it up and settling into the bench seat.

I was reading when someone knocked on my window, scaring the crap out of me. Jag was standing outside my car, a dumb smile on his perfect face. I rolled it down and looked at him, hoping the bored expression on my face was as cute and aloof as I thought it was.

"How's it goin', doll face?" he slurred, winking at me in an exaggerated manner. His breath reeked of alcohol.

"Please tell me you don't plan on driving that," I said, motioning to his motorcycle, which was parked up ahead. "You really shouldn't be operating a motor vehicle while intoxicated." I mused.

"Then take me home," he winked, a smirk on his face.

"God, I don't want to feel responsible for you dying tonight. Get in," I groaned, rolling up the window.

"Whatever you say, honey," he slurred. He all but stumbled over to the passenger side. I sighed and gripped the wheel.

"How drunk are you?" I asked as I pulled out of my spot and on to the road.

"Drunk," he laughed, looking out the window, "You know those giant handles of rum? Yeah, I topped one of those," he said proudly. I smiled slightly and shook my head, *boys*.

"What are you even supposed to be?" I asked, looking at him. He was wearing a pair of black jeans and a black button down. He pointed to the front of his collar and I saw a small white band. "A priest?" I laughed, and he laughed with me.

"Sure," he shrugged, pulling at the band, which turned out to be a blank white folded note card taped under the lapels of his shirt. I couldn't stop laughing. He was ridiculous, especially in this inebriated state. "It was Kent's idea, I don't do the whole costume thing," he said, settling into the seat, tilting his head against the window. I pulled up to a four-way intersection and looked at him.

"Where am I going?"

"Past the tracks, trailer park off Leland Street," he said, mumbling the last part. I drove to the trailer park and he gave me the number. I pulled up to a muddy, dented metal trailer and parked out front.

"Here we are," I nodded, looking over at him. He was half slumped against the door, forehead pressed against the window. He straightened up and nodded. He looked at me, then his eyes traveled down my body. I was suddenly aware of how little I was wearing. He smiled a wry smile—he was very good at that—and pinched my thin boxer shorts between his thumb and pointer finger, feeling the thin, well-worn fabric.

"Nice," he nodded, before getting out of the car and closing the door. I scoffed, it seemed to always be zero to 60 with him, I never knew which version of Jagger I was going to get. This realization made me mad, I was ready to drive away, leaving him in a cloud of dust when I saw him struggling to get his key in the lock. I sighed, got out, locked my truck, and walked over. I unlocked the door and he walked in, tripped on his backpack, and fell.

"You're a messy drunk," I groaned as I walked in, stepping over him to get into the small kitchen. He grunted from the floor, it almost sounded like a chuckle.

"Welcome to my home, it sucks," he said trying to reach the counter to help himself up, instead he grabbed the handle of a frying pan left on the small stove. I caught it right before it hit him in the head. I helped him up and steadied him.

"Come on, let's get you to bed, sleep this off." I sighed, making sure he was stable before letting go of his arm.

I looked around the small trailer, across from the door was a dingy little kitchen, to the left was a thin wall with an open door, to the right was another thin wall, the open door exposing a small bathroom. Through the first door there was a mattress on the floor, a ratty old blanket and one pillow laid haphazardly on top of it, the fitted sheet was untucked from one of the corners. Clothes littered the floor and the bed.

"You look fine tonight," he said, leaning against a wall, a move that would have been suave if he hadn't just almost accidentally knocked himself out with a frying pan.

"Come on, I need to be back at that party to pick up my sister." I groaned, pulling my jacket sides together.

"Hang out here for a little, we can make out," he put his hand on my waist, pulling me closer. I pushed him away, scoffing at his audacity. I was still unsure about my feelings for him, and right now they were sliding more towards the negative side of the scale than the positive.

"Sleep this off," I repeated, pointing to the bedroom. "Come on, Jag," I sighed, pulling him into the bedroom.

"Going to the bedroom so soon, hot," he smiled, pulling me into him, his hands on my waist. Our bodies were pressed against each other, noses were centimeters apart.

"I'm not hooking up with you," I said taking a step back.

"Fine, then leave," he spat, dropping his leather jacket on the floor.

"Fine, just don't drink anymore, or drive anywhere," I snapped, getting ready to go.

"Don't worry, I can't even afford beer at the moment anyways," he said unbuttoning his shirt. He dropped it on the ground and kicked off his boots. The sudden motion of removing his boots made him stagger back then fall back against the wall.

"Then why do you live on your own, why not with your parents?" I asked, crossing my arms, intrigued at the whole situation.

"Because. And your boobs look great like that," he smiled at me.

"Don't piss me off," I uncrossed my arms and pulled the sides of my jacket together again.

"Right, anger problems," he laughed, undoing his jeans. I wanted to kill Dani for letting that little fact slip in the auto shop. And him right now for being a drunk idiot.

"Hey shut up, I'm working on it." My cheeks were burning.

"Yeah and how many therapists and anger management coaches have you had?" he flicked a cigarette into his mouth and dropped his jeans. He was wearing tight black boxer briefs. Why was I still here humoring him?

"Shut up, I'm leaving, don't burn the place down," I said, about to walk out.

"Why, will you miss me too much if I die?" he cooed. I groaned and scoffed at him. He lit the cigarette and sat on his makeshift bed, leaning against the wall.

After a few moments of silence, he smiled up at me and tilted his head to the side. "Come sit, let's talk," he said patting next to him on the bed. I laughed at the offer, tugging on the hem of my jacket. This was the weirdest night ever. I should just go, walk out, get in my truck, and leave. That would be the smart, rational thing to do. Right?

"I have to get Dani," I said, my hand on the door knob. However, somewhere, deep down inside, I was hoping he would tell me to stay anyways. My mind flashed to the tape and the lyrics on the envelope, I knew he left it for me. I hadn't said anything about it, and neither did he, but I knew it was him. After he did that, something about the past few weeks changed in my mind. How he acted, it changed things—like how the way I felt about him. I might actually like this guy. Then, after a long silence, he exhaled a cloud of smoke and looked at me.

"You can spare a half hour," he smiled and patted the bed again. I sighed and sat down on the edge of the mattress at the end of the bed.

"Well?" I said, staring at him. He looked at me, his eyes searching mine, and he pushed himself up slightly, leaning forward.

"You know, the first time I saw you, you know, when you kicked the door off your truck and it hit me? I was so pissed then I saw you, with your long brown hair, big brown eyes, those pretty pink lips, and your incredibly hot body. I felt, I don't even know, for the first time I actually had feelings, and not just 'I want to hook up with you feelings' but 'I might like this girl' feelings. But I had to keep up my tough guy act, so when you came into the auto shop I was so excited," he rambled, his hands on his annoyingly chiseled bare chest, cigarette hanging from his perfect lips. I couldn't believe what he was saying. I stayed silent, hoping he would go on.

"But then I couldn't let you know I was happy to see you so I pretended to go after your sister. Then Kent came and, and, I'm just an asshole," he sighed, taking my small hand in his big ones, "Long,

49

embarrassing story short—I think you're beautiful, and I know I've been a jerk these past couple of weeks, but I just, I get riled up around you," he put his cigarette out and stared into my eyes. "I don't know how to do this, you know, the whole feelings thing."

"And you're drunk," I sighed, reality hit me like a ton of bricks. I went to stand but he took my hands in his again.

"Seriously, Carter, you're gorgeous, and you're nice and I love it when you get angry and I love it how you're taking care of me and act like you hate me," he laughed slightly.

"Oh, stop it, now I really have to go get Dani," I groaned.

"Just kiss me," he smiled, caressing my cheek with his thumb.

"You're drunk and don't know what you're saying," I said, going to stand again.

"Wait!" he pulled me back down. I fell into his lap and we fell backwards onto his bed.

"I like this," he smiled, his hands on my back, slowly inching downward. "I swear, I really like you," he said, holding me closer. My arms were bent under me, pinned between our bodies, my hands were flat against his bare chest, and I thought about pushing myself up and leaving. But the way he was staring at me, his green eyes were so beautiful this close, I didn't know what to do. He tilted his head up and kissed me. I was stunned, kind of. He was an asshole. An asshole who might have just said some nice things, but that didn't excuse the last few weeks. I stopped him and pushed myself up. I wasn't sure about my feelings for him but this definitely wasn't helping. I needed to clear my head, get things and my feelings straight.

"Alright, I really have to go," I stood and pulled my jacket on.

"Come back after," he smiled, standing and taking my hips in his hands, sliding them up my sides and back down again.

"I have curfew," I sighed, "And you're drunk, that was just, I don't know." I raked my fingers through my hair, I needed to get out of here.

"Come over tomorrow," he said standing, taking my hand in his.

"You'll be hung over, you should just sleep it off," I sighed, tucking my hair behind my ears.

"So, I'll see you at school?" he asked, taking both my hands in his now, pulling me closer. I exhaled slowly, squeezed his hands, then let go.

"I will see you at school," I nodded, taking a step back. He sighed, his broad shoulders dropping slightly.

"Bye," I said walking out. I got in my truck and looked back at the trailer then sighed and drove away.

I drove back to the party and called Dani. A few minutes later she came out, kissed a boy, then all but skipped to the car.

"Who was that?" I asked as I drove home.

"My boyfriend," she said plainly, picking at her chipping nail polish.

"And since when do you have a boyfriend?" I laughed.

"Since tonight," she smiled. I rolled my eyes and shook my head.

"So where were you? Mason and I went outside and I didn't see the truck."

"I got food," I lied casually.

"You were with Jag, weren't you?!" she squealed, clearly intoxicated.

"No," I said defensively.

"Then why are you wearing his jacket?" she pinched the beat-up leather.

"Shit," I groaned.

"You guys hooked up didn't you!" she laughed, clapping her hands.

"He kissed me," I admitted, unsure why I was telling her this. Maybe I just needed to say it out loud, to make sure that the last hour had really just happened. "I guess I grabbed the wrong jacket."

"It smells good," she said sniffing it.

"It smells like smoke and booze," I said, inhaling the faded, beat up leather.

"The scent of a real man," she said goofily.

"You're drunk," I laughed.

"Just a bit," she smiled a dumb smile and sat back.

I parked and we went upstairs and she went to bed right away. I went over to my desk and carefully folded his jacket over the back of the chair and got into bed. I couldn't help but replay the night's events over and over again in my mind. Him coming up to my window a drunken mess, laughing together in the car, the messy entrance to his trailer, the whole conversation that followed. And then there was the kiss. That kiss. My heart beat faster as I thought about it. Maybe it could work between us, maybe he was telling the truth about how he felt. Maybe if I just embraced the feelings I felt and was open with him, it would all work out. I fell asleep thinking of what I would say to him tomorrow when I went to return his jacket, a smile on my face as I thought of the possibility that he actually felt the same way back.

I woke up around noon and changed into a pair of dark blue skinny jeans and a sweatshirt, grabbed my keys and Jag's jacket and got in my truck. I drove to the trailer park and parked outside his trailer. I looked in the rearview mirror, I wasn't wearing any make-up, and my hair was in loose, natural curls. I pinched my cheeks for some color and smiled at my reflection before getting out and walking over. I knocked on the door and no one answered. I knocked again and I heard a thud and grumbling from inside.

"What?" Jag grunted, opening the door. His skin was pale and waxy, big purple bags circled the underside of his tired, bloodshot eyes. "Oh, it's you."

"Oh, it's me?" I repeated, confused.

"Is this yours?" he grabbed my jacket off the counter.

"Yeah, and this is yours." I handed him his jacket.

"Why, again, were you here last night?" he asked as he leaned against the door frame. His elbow was against the frame, and he scratched the back of his head. His stained, white tank top rose and exposed the prominently outlined 'V' that led to his loose hanging sweat pants.

"You don't remember anything from last night, do you?" I felt my stomach drop and mouth go dry.

"Not really, but please, enlighten me of my drunken disaster," he motioned for me to come in. I walked in and he closed the door and walked into his bedroom. He sat on the bed and lit a cigarette. "So, what happened, all I remember is going to some party and a handle of rum," he said, a half smile on his face. I stood at the end of his mattress, arms crossed over my chest.

"Well, you came up next to me, smashed out of your mind, I told you shouldn't be driving while you were drunk so I drove you here. You're a really messy drunk by the way," I said, leaning against the doorframe to the bedroom. "Then, you told me that you had feelings for me and all but begged me to kiss you. After we did, you begged me to come back after I dropped Dani off."

He laughed and looked at me, his eyes were sparkling with amusement. When I met his be-musement with a look that clearly read as 'I'm not kidding', he took a shaky drag then stood.

"Shit, are you serious?"

I nodded and smiled a tight smile. This was all wrong. I shouldn't have come here, or let myself have feelings for this asshole.

"Fuck. You didn't tell anyone what I said, right?" He took another shaky drag, pacing in the small room.

"No, don't worry, your secret is safe with me," I said before grabbing my jacket and walking out.

"Wait!" he, grabbed my hand, twirling me back into him. Our bodies were pressed together now, faces inches from each other. I had *déjà vu* from last night.

"Why do you have to take everything so literally?" he said, a hint of whine in his voice.

"Well that was pretty simple." I breathed. We were quiet for a few seconds, bodies still pressed together, he leaned down and kissed me greedily.

"You are so bipolar!" I all but yelled, pushing myself off him.

"At least I'm not the one with anger issues!" he said, just as loud. I couldn't help it, I slapped him across his gorgeous face and stormed out of the small trailer, the door slamming against the metal siding behind me. I got in my truck, slamming the door shut and drove off, leaving him standing in the doorway rubbing his reddening cheek.

Chapter Five

Jagger

*I*t was a cold November morning and I was stuck in bumper-bumper traffic on my bike on my way to school. I was freezing and sick of this shit. I dropped my cigarette on the pavement and took backroads all the way to school. As I rode through the parking lot, I saw Carter and Dani get out of Carter's truck. I looked at her, she was wearing skin tight gray jeans, a long-sleeved shirt, her black leather jacket, and a pair of lace up boots. A long, maroon knit scarf was wrapped around her neck.

She looked gorgeous as ever, her hair in a loose knot, a few strands hanging on either side of her perfect face. I sighed, she was perfect for me and I screwed it all up. It had been nearly month since the whole ordeal with her at my trailer, and we hadn't talked since. She even moved seats in Eaton's class. I needed to do something to put me back in her head, and before I even committed to the plan I sped over and parked right in front of her path.

"Watch it, asshole!" she yelled, stopping short by my side.

"What are you going to do about it?" I teased, taking my helmet off and getting off my bike. She was fuming now.

"Breathe," Dani said, pulling Carter away from me. I smiled and shook my head and walked in the other way.

I waited till everyone was in Eaton's class before walking in. Carter was sitting on the opposite side of the room from where we used to sit. I walked up to the kid in the seat next to her, stared at him, and he grabbed his stuff and moved. I sat and she looked at me with an annoyed look.

"You already used that move, go back to your playbook, Hastings," she said.

"Why knock a move when it's proven to work?" I shrugged. She scoffed and looked forward. Eaton went up to close the door and surveyed the class. His eyes fell on me, then moved to Carter. He smirked and went over to the board.

"Just an FYI, it doesn't work, at least not on me," she whispered. I looked at her and she hadn't even looked at me, not once. "You're going to have to do a lot better to get in my good graces." She was facing forward, eyes on the board. I sighed and looked forward too.

At lunch, I walked through the cafeteria straight to the courtyard. I didn't even bother looking for anyone to sit with, I always ate alone outside so I could smoke. Once I got outside I put my tray down, sat at one of the tables, and lit a cigarette. I took a long drag and exhaled the smoke out through my nose.

"You know that will kill you," Carter said, walking out and sitting at a table on the other end of the courtyard.

"We all die eventually, so what if I'm just speeding up the process?" I said plainly.

"Beautiful, very poetic," she said sarcastically before taking a bite of her salad.

"I was thinking of taking up a career in poetry," I said coolly, taking another long drag.

"Oh, how interesting, please do tell me more," she shot back. I smiled, stood, and walked over, sitting down across from her. I looked at her for a long time before finally asking her the question that had been burning my brain for weeks.

"Why did you hit me when I kissed you?"

"I don't like it when people bring up my issues," she looked at her salad.

"Well you called me bipolar!" I laughed, taking one last drag before putting the cigarette out.

"Because you are." she looked up at me. I didn't know what to say, my mind went blank. Shit, I must really like her, and that thought made me feel weird.

"Yeah, well, I'm not," was all I could come up with.

"Oh, wow! Good comeback, top notch, really," she laughed as she packed up her bag. She got up and walked over to the trash can, throwing her food out. I needed a Hail Mary move—and then I got one. Hoping it would work, I stood, walked over, and kissed her again. This time it was soft and sweet. I curved one hand around her cheek and neck, the other on her hip. She loosely gripped my sides and slowly started to kiss me back. The bell rang and she jumped back.

"I have to get to class," she grabbed her bag and ran off. I sighed and smiled, shaking my head. This chick was crazy and I was undeniably falling in love with her.

I decided to blow off gym, instead I sat on my bike, chain smoking and thinking about what to do. Finally, the last bell rang and I waited till I saw Carter. She was laughing—why was she laughing when she wasn't with anyone? Then I saw who she was with, some tall preppy tool. I felt the urge to go punch him in the face, but she wasn't my girlfriend. I couldn't just go and do that. What if I had missed my chance? What if I had truly screwed it up this time, and she was gone? I groaned and pulled on my helmet. I sighed, revved my engine, and sped home. I locked my bike up and went inside.

I laid in bed that night thinking about Carter. I couldn't think about anything else, she was on my mind nearly every second of every day since I met her. I never felt like this before, so why did I have to be such an asshole? I sighed and sat up and lit a cigarette. It was my last one. I groaned, I'd have to go get more tomorrow before school.

I let out a long, body racking sigh and looked at the grate covering the air vent by my bed. I got up and went over to my jacket and took out my wallet, even though I knew nothing would be in it. I looked anyways, determined to be sure that what I was about to do was the ultimate last resort. When I finally came to terms with my decision, I lifted the air vent and grabbed the envelope in it. I held it in my hands for a long time before I flipped open the top. I took out a $20 bill, and then looked at the bills in there: my parent's money. I felt sick using it, but I couldn't find real work between school, the garage, and the occasional shift at Frank's bar. I sat back and counted how much was left. It wasn't much. I groaned, knowing what was going to have to happen soon, and hating the very thought of it.

I sealed the envelope, taped it back to the side, and closed the vent, putting the $20 in my jacket pocket. I laid back, finished my cigarette, then fell asleep thinking of Carter.

Chapter Six

Carter

I was sitting at my desk doing homework when there was a knock on my door. I knew Dad wasn't home and Dani never knocked. I got up, confused, and opened it. Dani was standing there in her pajamas, wringing her fingers.

"Can I come in?" She asked softly.

"What's up?" I asked, moving so she could walk in. Something was wrong. She never knocked, or came to my room just to talk. Not since we were kids. She walked in and sat on the edge of my bed, pulling her knees to her chest. I stood at the edge of my bed and looked at her, curled up with her arms around her legs. I waited for her to speak, and she looked at me then off to the side before she did.

"So, Mason and I had sex," she said slowly. I sat on my bed and looked at her. She tucked her face into the crook between her knees. I sat with one knee bent, the other hanging over my bed so I could face her.

"Okay…" I said. Dani and I were not ones for sisterly moments like this. She would always go to Mom to talk about things, and I to Dad. I guess I was all she had left since Mom passed.

"Well, he didn't wear a condom," she said slowly, and I groaned. I knew where this was going.

"Oh, Dani," I whispered, rubbing my forehead.

"I don't know anything for sure yet, Carter. I just know I'm 5 days late," she said, getting defensive. I sighed and patted her shoulder. The display of affection felt forced, but the right thing to do. I thought for a long time then blew out a long, exasperated breath.

"I'm not mad, I'm just, well, I'm mad at him. I'm going to kick that kid's ass." I said, thinking about her boyfriend Mason. His perfectly coiffed blond hair, dumb, vacant look on his overly pretty face. How his outfits always seemed so perfect, he probably planned them out a week in advance. All of these thoughts fueled my anger towards him.

"And as for you, we'll get you a test first thing in the morning," I said, squeezing her shoulder softly. She nodded and tucked her chin in the crook between her two knees. Tears pooled in the corners of her eyes.

"I feel so stupid," she whispered, a sob slipped out and she covered her mouth then looked away from me. I sighed and rubbed her back, something Mom used to do. She put her face in her knees and cried for a couple minutes.

"We'll figure it out, we always do. Remember what Mom always used to say?" I smiled. She tilted her head back and wiped her eyes, smiling a tight smile.

"Us Baker girls have to stick together," we both said in unison. I smiled and nodded. A pang of sadness hit me right in my chest, but I pushed it back down.

"That's right, and we will," I said. She smiled and wiped her nose.

"Do you miss her?" She asked. I sighed and nodded.

"Of course, I do. But she was so sick for so long," I said softly. Dani nodded and closed her eyes.

"I'm scared I'm going to forget her." She admitted after a long silence. "I mean, Dad was so gung-ho on leaving Oregon after she died. It's like, my only memories of her are there," she said softly.

"You'll never forget her, Dani, she's our mom. And Dad needed to get out of that house and start fresh. It was so much harder on him than us, and he had dealt with it for much longer. A fresh start and a clean break were going to be the only way he could keep going," I said, knowing Dad and why he made the choices he did. She nodded slowly.

"I know," she sighed, "And the job offer came at the right time, I'm not mad we're here, it's just-it's just different," she said. I nodded in agreement.

"It'll be okay," I said, nudging her with my foot. She nodded, cleaned herself up, composed herself, and stood.

"Thanks, Car," she said before leaving. I sighed and laid down, rubbing my eyes. I honestly had not thought about Mom in a long time. She was a sore subject for both Dad and me. Dani always got along so well with her, Dani was her baby. Her perfect child, no issues—nothing to make her think about her own issues. The same issues that I struggled with, which she ultimately resented me for. Mom was a diagnosed manic depressive with bipolar tendencies, and anger issues—the latter a genetic chemical imbalance that she happily passed down to me, her accidental first born.

I got up and went over to my closet, dragging my chair over. I climbed up and grabbed the box stacked at the top. I pulled the photo album out of it and got down, sitting on the floor cross legged. I put it down in front of me and opened it slowly. The first photo was after I was born. Mom was in a hospital bed, blond hair tied up in a messy bun, loose pieces matted to her sweaty forehead. She was cradling me, Dad was standing next to her, his hand cupping my head. Both were looking at me, but only Dad was smiling.

I flipped the page and looked at all the childhood photos. They were mostly of me with Dad or me alone. Mom either took the photos—another trait I shared with her—or chose not to be in them. Then, Dani was welcomed into the world. I looked at the photo, it was just like mine, but entirely different. Mom in a hospital bed, this time her blond hair was in a messy braid, Dani in her arms, one hand cradling her, the other was on her chest, a finger caressing her chin. A perfect, maternal moment caught on camera, immortalized forever. Dad was standing behind her, holding me in his arms, I was two at the time.

We all looked so happy, nothing was truly wrong then. At least, Dani and I didn't really know what was going on behind the closed door of their bedroom. The post-partum after I was born did a number on her, and subsequently Dad. Then, she could finally go back on her medication after she weened me onto formula, she soon after got pregnant with Dani, forcing her to go off her medication again. The chemical imbalance wracked her mentally, and caused her to fall deeper into her depression.

Childhood was not fun in the Baker household with a mother who rarely left bed. Dad had just landed his attending position at the hospital, which meant he was rarely around, leaving Dani and I with a ticking time bomb at home. I spent every moment I could either locked in my room or out of the house. This caused Dani and me to drift. She worshipped Mom, and resented me for hating her as much as I did.

When I was 16 and Dani was 14, Mom got worse. Her manic episodes increased and grew longer and more frequent, her medication stopped controlling the anger issues, and Dad got worried for our safety. He made arrangements to check her into a facility. But that never happened. She cleared out the ample medicine cabinet, locked herself in the bathroom, and that was the end of it.

I slammed the photo album closed and shoved it back in the box, putting it back where I had it hidden before and closed the doors to the closet. I couldn't go back there, let those thoughts crowd my mind like they did in the past. I needed to be done with her, get her out of my mind once and for all.

Chapter Seven

Jagger

That morning I parked in front of the convenience store by school and took my helmet off. I couldn't believe it—Carter's truck was parked outside and Dani was sitting in the cab. Carter must be inside. I smiled to myself and walked in, looking for her. She was in one of the aisles reading the back of a small box. I walked over to the counter and asked for two packs Marlboro Ultras and handed him the $20.

"Shit," she sighed, trying to hide what she was buying behind her back.

"Miss, your purchase?" the man behind the counter said. She put a pregnancy test down on the counter and a small box of condoms.

"I guess I should stop trying to kiss you then, Mommy," I sighed before grabbing my cigarettes and walking out. She threw some money down on the counter and ran out after me. "They're not for me," she said, stopping a few feet away from me.

"Oh, really? Because I saw you pretty buddy-buddy with some asshole yesterday," I spat, getting on my bike.

"Yeah, that's my lab partner, my very gay lab partner, and these, they're for my sister. She's a dumbass who had unprotected sex with her boyfriend," She whisper-yelled as she came closer. I got off my bike and kissed her right there, pulling her in close. Her hands were pressed against my chest, they slowly went from fists to palms open and slightly gripping the lapels of my jacket.

"Get a room," Dani yelled from the truck.

"I should go," she breathed.

"Lunch, courtyard," I said before getting on my bike. I sped off, smiling to myself.

I walked out to the back courtyard and Carter was sitting there eating her salad. I walked over and put my cigarette out and kissed her. She laughed and swallowed her food.

"So, is there a bun in the oven?"

"No," she said, relief seeped through her tone. I smiled and looked at her. She was wearing overall shorts over black tights, a similar long sleeve shirt as yesterday, no leather jacket. This time it was a maroon, baggy knit cardigan, and her ever-present lace-up boots. She looked cute yet hot at the same time.

"So, how about you come over for dinner Friday night? We can order in Chinese and I don't know, hang out," I said, the last part slowly.

"Um sure, I think that could work," she said before slowly taking a bite of salad.

"Cool," I nodded. It was a very awkward exchange overall. We talked lightly the rest of lunch but then the bell rang and we stood. "See you Friday."

She nodded and tossed her salad in the garbage.

"See ya," she waved, slinging her backpack on her shoulder before leaving.

I wish I had kissed her, I'm such a dumbass.

I skipped out on my last period class and went over to my motorcycle. I saw Carter sitting on a fold up beach chair in the bed of her truck.

"What are you doing?" I asked as I walked over. I rested my arms on the side of the bed, looking at her with what I imagine was a dumb, love struck look.

"Skipping, didn't really feel like going through an hour of math without punching someone. I told the guidance counselor I was going to have an episode if I went to math, she gave me a pass," she said, tilting her head towards the faint sun. I laughed and rested my chin on my arms.

"You can join me, but only if you're skipping. If you have a free then you're not cool enough to sit with me," she joked. I smiled and jumped up on to the truck bed and unfolded the other chair.

"So why didn't you go to class?"

I popped a cigarette in my mouth and lit it, "I hate my English teacher, she's a bitch on wheels," I said exhaling into the cold crisp air. Carter giggled at the expression and I smiled.

I looked at Carter, she was wearing her leather jacket over her sweater, mittens, and a blanket on her lap. Her hair was stuffed into a loose hanging cap on the back of her head except for a few strands hanging on either side of her face. Her cheeks were cherry red from the cold.

"Can I have one?" she asked softly, taking a mitten off. I handed her a cigarette and lit it for her. She inhaled slowly and exhaled the smoke in slow, perfect circles.

"You smoke?" I laughed, in total disbelief of what I was seeing.

"Well, kinda," she sighed, rubbing her red-tipped nose softly, her cigarette masterfully placed between her fingers. She sat back, crossed her legs under the blanket and looked at the sky, "I dated a guy who did and I eventually picked it up. I try not to." she shrugged, taking another drag. I smiled and took one as well.

After a long span of silence, she turned and looked at me and asked, "So why is everyone scared of you?" I laughed and she just stared back at me.

"What stories have you heard?"

"You know the taste of animal blood," she smiled, smoke billowing out with every word. I laughed and leaned over, kissing her slowly, one hand on her thigh and the other on her cheek and neck. When we parted, her cheeks were redder than before. She took an even shakier drag then stubbed out her cigarette on the bottom of her boot. I smiled and put mine out and we continued kissing. The bell ran and kids started coming out of the school. I jumped off the back of her truck and offered my hand to her. She smiled at me and took it, jumping down.

"See you Friday," I said pulling her towards me, kissing her again. She nodded, a blissful look on her face. I kissed her cheek then walked over to my bike, got on, and rode home.

Friday night, I got back late from the auto garage and my place was a mess. I threw all the clothes that were on the floor of my bedroom into a pile in the corner and threw the covers over my bed more neatly, then cleaned up the bathroom a bit. There was a knock on the door and I smiled, opening the door.

"Hey," Carter smiled. She was wearing a pair of torn up skinny jeans, a sweater, and her hair was down, natural waves cascaded around her perfect face.

"Hey," I said, leaning down to kiss her. She kissed me quickly then I moved so she could come in. I took her coat, hung it on the hook by the door, then grabbed the Chinese food menu. We ordered and I got money out from the envelope in the vent while she was in the bathroom.

We sat cross-legged on my bed, our backs to the wall watching TV and talking casually. There was a small moment of silence before she spoke.

"You seem off ease," she said before biting a dumpling.

"I don't know, I've never really done this before," I said, swallowing a bite of my egg roll.

"What, a date?" she laughed. I nodded and she stopped laughing. "How have you never been on a date?"

"Well I've never had a date like this. Where we eat…" I said slowly.

"Oh." She blushed.

"Crap I ruined this, didn't I?" I groaned.

"No," she laughed putting her hand on my knee, "You're doing fine," she smiled.

I sighed and smiled. When we were done with dinner we cleared our plates and laid in bed facing each other. One of her arms was crooked under her head and the other one was tracing the patterns on my hand, which was palm down, flat on the bed.

"Why do you live in a trailer alone?" she asked softly. It had been a long time since either of us had spoken.

"A story for another time," I whispered back after an even longer silence. She nodded and leaned over and kissed me. I put my hand on her hip and pulled her waist and legs closer. She slowly moved on top of me and we kept kissing. I sat up and she fell back on the bed, laughing. I pulled my shirt over my head and leaned over her and kissed her again. She wrapped her legs around my waist and kissed my neck. I bit my lip, staring at her for a minute. God, she was beautiful. I smiled and kissed her again. There was banging on the door before it busted open with a loud bang, and my landlord Chuck barged in.

"Your rent's late," he spat, not even caring what was going on. He was a big guy, built like a linebacker, and took up the rest of the space in the small room.

"Jesus, Chuck, get the fuck out," I yelled.

"Your rent is over a week late," he said again, and I noticed the baseball bat in his hands.

"Here," I grabbed the envelope, taking the last of the money I had out. I got up and handed him the money.

"Thank you," he said coldly before leaving.

"Holy crap," Carter breathed, I turned and she was huddled as far back on the bed as she could be.

"Sorry," I said, kneeling on the bed, rubbing her biceps. Her eyes were still wide, her breathing rapid.

"It's late, I have curfew," she said getting up slowly.

"Aw come on, Carter," I groaned.

She moved to the end of the bed to pull on her boots.

"Stay, just for a little longer," I said, sitting behind her and kissing her shoulder. She smiled and kissed me before standing and pulling on her coat.

"See you on Monday," she said, zipping it up.

"See you Monday," I sighed, kissing her goodbye. I watched her get in her truck and drive away.

Chapter Eight

Jagger

On Monday, I was on my way to school when my phone buzzed. I stopped and looked at the screen, it was Carter.

"Hey."

"My truck broke down as I was pulling out of the driveway and my Dad's already at work. Can you come get me?" she asked in a rather reluctant tone.

"Sure, text me your address."

"Okay," she said then hung up. She sent me her address and I sighed, it was on the richer side of town. I sped over there and went down the long driveway to her house—a large white colonial with blue shutters, a wraparound porch, and a balcony in front of each second-floor window. She was standing outside, her bag by her feet, Ray Bans perched on her nose. I stopped in front of her and she slung her bag on her back and straddled the back of my bike.

"Hold on tight," I smiled. She wrapped her arms around my stomach and I sped off. We got to school and everyone stared as we got off and walked to class together.

"So, am I allowed to kiss you in public?" I asked, putting one hand on the wall by her hand and the other hooked in her belt loop.

"Yeah," she nodded, a coy smile on her lips, pulling me closer by my jacket. I leaned down and kissed her, curving my body into her. She held me closer and we kissed for a few more minutes before the bell rang and she pushed me off her.

"Bye," she laughed, going into her classroom. I sighed and smiled and went to class.

I sat outside and lit a cigarette and took a drag. Carter and I didn't have the same lunch period that day so I looked for her when I walked out of school at the end of the day. She was sitting on my bike.

"Hey," I smiled, sitting in front of her.

"Hi," she wrapped her arms around my waist.

"I'm going to have to take you straight home, I have to go somewhere." She nodded and I sped off. I dropped her off and she put her hands on my shoulders and kissed me.

"My truck isn't going to be fixed till Wednesday," she said slowly.

"I'll pick you up tomorrow," I smiled, kissing her before revving my engine.

I sped down the familiar roads and up to the large, wrought iron gate. I stopped, sitting on my bike for a long time. I finally let out a long sigh, punched in the code, and waited for the tall gate to slowly swing open. I drove up the long, winding, tree-lined driveway and up to the house. Well, it wasn't exactly a house, it was an old Tudor mansion with pristine upkeep. The large shrubs and bushes were trimmed to perfection, the sprawling lawn was currently being mowed, and there was a small crew in the garage washing the cars. Trina wouldn't have it any other way.

I walked up to the door and sighed, scuffing my boots against the marble entryway. I went to knock but sighed and took a step back. I needed this, there was no true other way. I opened the double doors and walked directly into the lion's den. Maids were silently scurrying about, none of them paid any attention to me. I walked further into the house and down to her office. I opened the door and she looked up from her desk.

"Jason, what are you doing here?" she gasped, dropping her cell phone on the desk.

"I need more money," I sighed, sliding my hands into my pockets.

"Of course, it's been a few months," she nodded, slightly disappointed. She slid out from behind her large, mahogany desk and straightened her skirt. She walked over to the large Van Gogh on the far wall and tugged gently on the frame. The painting swung back on hidden hinges and exposed her sizeable wall safe. She punched in the combo and the safe popped open with a loud, metallic squeal—piercing the silence in the room. She smoothed her blond, shoulder length hair and looked over her shoulder at me.

"How much this time, 5?" she asked, looking back at the bundles of cash stacked neatly within the safe. I shrugged and she took out $5,000 and handed it to me. I stuffed it in my jacket's inside pocket and ran my fingers through my hair.

"I thought you were finally coming home," she admitted sheepishly, straightening the sleeves of her blouse.

"Yeah well, not while he's still here," I said, involuntarily looking at the giant family portrait against the wall behind her desk. It was a formal painting, done many years ago—but I could remember the day like it was yesterday. My father and mother stood behind a young Juliet and I, their hands behind their backs, not embracing us like normal parents do.

However, before it was painted, Juliet had locked herself in her bathroom for four hours, refusing to sit for the painting, and I took a buzzer to my perfectly coiffed hair, giving myself a mohawk. Jason Sr. was so mad he not only made the painter change my hair, but he made us sit for six hours while the man painted us, even though the artist insisted he could work off a photograph. Then, after it was all said and done, he enrolled me in military school and Juliet in an all-girls private school.

Trina sighed and looked at me with a forlorn look. "He misses you, we all do, especially Juliet," she said softly.

"He probably doesn't even know I'm gone," I laughed, "And Juliet's a big girl," I sighed.

She wrinkled her nose ever so slightly and blew out a long sigh. She restored the painting and sat back down at her desk. "Well, what's new with your life?" she pried, trying to keep me there longer.

"Nothing." The money was already burning a hole in my pocket, and not in a good way.

"Juliet's friends at your school said they've seen you with a girl, who is she?"

"No one."

"Alright," she sighed, defeated.

"I've got to go." I left as quickly as I came.

"Bye," she called out as I made my quick escape. I heard the door slam and Juliet ran in.

"Holy shit, you are here!" she said, excitedly hugging me.

"Hey," I said softly, slowly hugging her back.

"Are you coming home?" she tugged on her plaid private school uniform skirt.

"No, just getting money."

"Oh," she pouted and crossed her arms. "So, when can I see your place?" she said, perking up.

"Not yet," I looked down.

"And the girl?"

"No, I have to go."

"When will I see you again?" she called as I walked out.

"I don't know," I said, waving her off.

"I miss my big brother," she said from the doorway.

"I'm sorry Juliet, but things change and shit happens," I sighed, lighting a cigarette.

"I thought you quit," her eyes were wide.

"I didn't quit, I just moved out," I said simply, turning to look at her.

She looked so broken and small. She was standing on the marble steps, arms crossed, nearly hugging herself. She was wearing a crisp white button down, gray cardigan with the school crest stitched into the right side, a plaid skirt, tights, and black flats. Her long black hair was half pinned back and wavy, and her face had matured. When I really looked at her, she looked older, more like Trina.

"Do you have to be anywhere?" she asked, walking outside.

"No," I sighed, taking a drag.

"Hang out with me, please, for a little," she begged.

"Fine, only a little," I sighed.

"Cigarette out," she said, blocking the door. I huffed a sigh, took one more long drag and stomped it out on the marble step up to the house.

"Thank you," she smiled. I growled at her and she laughed and went up the large, curved staircase. She opened the double doors to her bedroom and walked in.

"Nice, uh, decorations," I tried, staring at the purple and green décor.

"Thanks," she smiled. I nodded and walked over to where the couches were and sat.

"So, who's the girl?" she said, sitting across from me. She sat so gracefully, tucking her long legs under herself. She had grown up in the time I had been gone.

"Just a girl from school," I said, already craving a cigarette.

"And?"

"What?" I sighed.

"Well Caroline and Katie saw you two getting off your bike and kissing outside in the halls and having lunch together," she sped-talked like she always did when she's nervous. I stood and went on her balcony and lit a cigarette. She followed me out and leaned against the railing.

"I don't know, I like her."

"Yeah?" she smiled, nodding encouragingly. I shrugged and nodded, playing it off like it was nothing.

"Do I know her?"

"No, she just moved here," I said. She nodded and smiled at me.

"You finally have a girlfriend," she said, her smile growing even wider.

"Shut up," I laughed. She stuck her tongue out at me and I smiled.

I heard a door slam and we both looked over the balcony wall. Jason Sr. had gotten out out of his convertible, and was now staring at my bike. Juliet squeaked an 'oh crap,' he then looked up and saw me. I put my cigarette out on the edge of the balcony and tore out of the room.

"When will I see you next?" Juliet called after me.

"I don't know," I sighed, looking at her one last time before I sped down the stairs.

"Jason," he said, standing in the doorway. I pushed past him and got on my bike.

"Jason!" he called after me as I sped off. I went straight to my home and slammed the door closed. I lit a cigarette and inhaled a shaky drag. I hated him.

Chapter Nine

Juliet

I stood on the foot of the steps of the grand staircase in the foyer, staring at the back of my Dad's head. His black hair was going gray, giving him a distinguished salt-and-pepper look. He was wearing a fitted navy blue suit, his black leather briefcase still gripped in his fist. He turned and looked at me.

"Why did you have to come home?" I said, choking back tears, "He was spending time with me, he was here!" I cried, hot tears rolling down my cheeks. He looked up at me, his green eyes were wide, but his face didn't give off any other emotion. He looked to his left, and I followed his gaze. Mom was standing at the entryway under the curve of the large staircase, her blue eyes were rimmed red. She had been crying.

He looked at her, then at me, then he blew out a long, exasperated sigh, tightened his tie, and walked off in the direction of his home office. I looked at Mom, but she had already turned back towards her own office. I sighed and tromped up the stairs. I went to my room, my hand on the knob, then I turned and looked across the hall at the double doors leading to Jason's room. I walked across the hall and opened the doors, walking in slowly.

Mom hadn't let any of the maids change anything in the room since Jason had left, leaving it like a shrine to him, and subsequently his absence. The room was large, a little larger than mine and with more windows. The whole far wall was floor to ceiling windows, looking out of the large, expansive back yard—the door to the balcony sat between all the windows. To my right was his king bed—it sat in a large, four-poster, mahogany frame. At the end of the bed was a chest with a large TV on it. By the windows there was a set of sofas facing one another, a small coffee table between them.

I walked into his bathroom, the cold marble floor under my bare feet sending chills through my body. I looked at the counter—it was bare, as were the large cabinets. He had a free-standing tub, the one thing I liked about his room more than mine, a large glass shower, and a private cubicle where the toilet was. Beyond the bathroom was the walk-in closet, also nearly empty. The only clothes left were things that he never wore—suits for functions that Mom and Dad made us go to, expensive pairs of pants, some still with the tags on them, and rows of button downs, sweaters, and fancy shirts, most untouched. The wall of shoes was neatly stocked with various colors and styles of loafers, dress shoes, sneakers, and boots. Only the boots and sneakers showed some sort of wear on them. I picked up a dark grey crew neck sweater that Jason used to wear around the house Sunday mornings and brought the fabric to my nose. It smelled just faintly of him. I pulled it on over my uniform and rolled up the long sleeves.

I walked out and over to his large, mahogany desk, still littered with classwork from years ago. I smiled, he had a small framed photo of me on his desk, a school photo from middle school. Then, a pang of sadness hit. This photo was here, not currently with him. A fresh wave of sadness rolled through me and I left the room, closing the double doors behind me with a slam. I stormed across the wide hallway and over to my own room. I walked in and smiled at the comfortable, safe space. My room was lived in, the bed—albeit made—was covered in personalized throw pillows and blankets, my schoolbag opened on it, the contents spread across the purple comforter. I had a large, white wrought iron bed frame, and draped over the bars were scarves and some clothes.

I glanced at my closet, it was overflowing with my clothes, shoes, and accessories. My walls were covered with photos of me and my friends. I sighed, sinking into an oversized, overstuffed leather club chair, thinking about how different Jason's life was now from what it was when he lived here, when he was a part of our family.

At 6 P.M. sharp I was downstairs in the dining room, sitting at my place at the long, ornate mahogany table. From my seat, I looked across the wide table from me at Jason's empty chair and sighed. To my left, about 5 feet down the table was Mom. She was sipping red wine from a large wine glass, the stem thin and long. To my right, another 5 feet down, was Dad. He had a crystal tumbler of scotch, and was knocking the ice around the glass with small, flicking movements from his fingers. A maid came out, followed by another, then one more. Each placed our food in front of us, I smiled and thanked mine, then looked at the perfectly crafted plate of food. I looked at Dad, as did Mom, and he looked at us, nodded, and we all began to eat.

We ate in silence for a while, as we always did, every night. Dad tapped his finger to the rim of his glass, and a maid walked over quickly, a bottle of 20-year-old scotch in one hand, a silver ice bucket in the other. She carefully put four ice cubes in his glass, poured three fingers of scotch, then took both back to the small bar in the corner. A few minutes passed then Mom held up her wine glass, and a different maid hurried over with an expensive bottle of wine and poured the deep, red liquid into her glass. The maid went to leave but she brought her back over with a single look, and held her glass up again. The maid poured more wine into her glass and Mom smiled a tight smile and nodded. I looked at them, first at Mom, then Dad, and I sighed, setting my silverware down.

"I miss Jason," I said.

"Juliet," Mom admonished, giving me a terse look, her eyes darting towards Dad. He cleared his throat and looked at his plate, his wife, then me.

"I know you do, Juliet," he said, cutting a piece of duck carefully before bringing it to his mouth.

"So why can't he come back?" I asked. I could feel Mom's eyes burning a hole in my side.

"He doesn't want to come back," Dad said, taking another bite of duck.

"Sebastian did an excellent job with this duck," Mom said, trying to change the subject. Dad nodded in agreement and began to cut a carrot.

"Are these from the garden?" he asked her, looking at the speared carrot on his fork. She smiled and nodded.

"Picked this morning," she stated quite proudly.

"This is bullshit!" I spat, banging my hand down on the table. Mom's eyes went wide and Dad put his fork and knife down carefully.

"We do not use that type of language, Juliet, please apologize to your mother and excuse yourself," he said, calmly.

"Or what, you'll kick me out too?" I shouted, standing up so quickly that the large wooden king-back chair scraped back and nearly toppled over.

"Young lady!" Mom said, in shock.

"Juliet Penelope Hastings, your room, now!" Dad boomed, slamming his fist on the table. The silverware, dishes, and glasses clattered and clinked, and a candle holder with a long, red, unlit taper in it, fell over, the candle split in the middle.

"Gladly!" I shouted back, storming off to my bedroom.

A few hours later I decided I needed to apologize, so I went upstairs to my parent's floor. Their bedroom was the entire third floor of the house—everything was over the top with them. When I came up the stairs and onto the landing, I looked around.

I rarely went up there, and when I did I always forgot how elaborate their living quarters were.

The space was spacious and open, the back wall, like Jason's, was all floor to ceiling windows with a door to the balcony in the center. In the middle of the room, with its back towards the wall of windows, was their bed. It was a huge California king on top of a platform. The frame was like Jason's, but more grandiose and intricate. On either side was a matching night stand, a lamp, and clock. The left side was Mom's, off on her side was a small cluster of matching couches with perfectly picked and placed throw pillows on them. All of this sat on a large, oriental area rug. Beyond that was her own bathroom and walk in closet. The right side was Dad's, he had the same set up, only curated towards his décor choices.

I was about to walk into the space when I heard a faucet shut off and Mom call out from her bathroom. The door was open, as was Dad's bathroom door.

"You can't blame her, dear," she said.

"I know, Trina, but I don't like when she talks to me like that, especially about Jason," Dad called from his bathroom. I sunk to the floor at the top of the steps and listened to them.

"She misses her big brother, she's 14. What do you expect from the girl?" she asked, her voice carrying towards his bathroom.

"The boy came at me with a broken wine bottle, Trina, he lunged at me! Like some kind of animal! I know I said some things as well, but the blatant disrespect, the violence, the audacity of his actions," he called, walking to the doorframe of his bathroom, toothbrush in hand. He was wearing a white t-shirt and blue pajama bottoms. He looked towards Mom's bathroom, and I carefully hid out of sight. I saw her step into the doorway of her bathroom, she was in a white silk pajama set.

"Yes, that was a turbulent time, and yes, you both acted rashly, but he is our son, *your* son. You gave him your name, you raised him, and then you kicked him out and took him away from your daughter, and from me, might I add," she said, her hands on his slim hips. Dad sighed and looked at her.

"I miss my son, Jason," she said, giving him a look before going back into her bathroom. Dad retreated to his bathroom in defeat and I stood, straightening my plaid pajama pants and white long sleeve shirt before walking into the room. I knocked on the frame of Dad's bathroom door.

"Dad?"

"Yes Juliet," He said, looking at me. He was rinsing his toothbrush in the sink.

"I am sorry about my behavior at dinner," I said. He looked at me and smiled a tight smile.

"Thank you, Juliet," he nodded.

"I do miss him, though, Dad," I said softly before leaving quietly, Dad speechless behind me.

Chapter Ten

Carter

*J*agger and I had been semi exclusively dating for about four months now and tonight was the first time he was meeting my Dad. I heard his motorcycle before I saw him. I looked out my window while I was getting ready and saw him park, take a final drag from his cigarette, put it out, then pace for a little before he knocked on the door. I smiled and pulled on my jeans and boots before grabbing my leather jacket and running downstairs. Dad was standing in the doorway, his arms crossed and Jag was still standing outside.

"Dad, have you met Jagger?" I smiled, putting my arm around my Dad. He looked Jag up and down. He was wearing a pair of jeans, a black long sleeve t-shirt with three buttons going down at the neck, and his leather jacket.

"Yes," he said tersely. Dad was very overprotective of Dani and I—boys weren't allowed in our rooms, or over past 10 P.M., and he had a very puritan hope that we were both still virgins. She and I had an unspoken mutual understanding that we would let him think that thought for as long as we could get away with. I looked at Jag and his body language was openly uncomfortable. I smiled, this was the first parent of a girl he had ever met. I put my hand on my Dad's back and he looked down at me, then at Jag.

"Why don't you come in for some coffee?" Dad offered, and I gave Jag a small smile and he nodded. He walked in and we followed my Dad to the kitchen. Jag and I sat at the kitchen table and Dad made a pot of coffee.

"So, Jagger," he said, Jag's name sounding weird coming from my Dad, "What do you do outside of school?" he asked as he worked on preparing the coffee.

"Well, I work in the school's auto body shop and sometimes I pick up shifts at a local bar," he said, his knee grazing mine under the table.

"A bar? How old are you?" Dad asked, obviously surprised.

"I'm 17, sir, but the owner has kind of taken me under his wing. He lets me cook and stock and move heavy stuff," Jag said, and Dad nodded at this, having processed the information and deeming it reasonable.

"And the auto body shop, maybe you could help Carter here with her truck. The damn thing keeps breaking down but she won't let me help her get a new car," He smirked, pouring three mugs off coffee.

"I love my truck and it works just fine!" I laughed, crossing my arms.

"That thing is a death trap, I've been bugging her to let me work on it but she is a stubborn girl," Jag said, bumping his knee against mine and I heard my Dad chuckle.

"That she is," he smiled, carrying the mugs over.

"And what are your plans for after high school?" Dad said, sipping from his mug.

"School has never really been my thing," Jag admitted, and Dad looked up at him, eyes weary. "Frank, the bar owner, has offered me a full-time job for after I graduate."

"No college?" Dad said, glancing at me then at Jag. Jag shrugged.

"Why waste the money when I could save it by working?" Jag said simply. Dad contemplated this then nodded slowly.

"Unorthodox but I appreciate the work ethic," he said, and Jag smiled. I could feel Jag's legs bouncing up and down, obviously anxious, and I smiled at my Dad.

"Dad, he and I should get going, but maybe we could all have dinner together some time, you could get to know each other better," I said, smiling at both of them. He nodded and we went back to the door. We walked outside and Dad looked past Jag, his eyes falling on his motorcycle.

"You didn't tell me he drives a motorcycle," he looked at me with *that* look. I smiled and squeezed his bicep.

"Don't worry, Dad, I've been on it before," I winked, laughing before kissing his cheek and walking out. Jag got on and I wrapped my arms around him. I looked back at my Dad and he had a small smile on his face. My mom used to ride a motorcycle, and seeing them made him think of her.

I blew him a kiss and he smiled, catching it. He nodded at me before closing the door behind him. Jag passed me my helmet and put his own on after.

"I need to make one stop," He said, turning his bike on.

"Ok, where?"

"Just a house," he said gruffly before speeding off.

He drove in to the very rich part of town and stopped in front of a huge iron gate. He punched in a code, a buzzer sounded, then the gate slowly opened. He rode up a long, tree-lined path to a huge Tudor mansion. The house was brick with dark trim and tall windows. There was a large, three car garage off to the side of the house. The doors were open and in it was a vintage Aston Martin, a large, sleek black Mercedes SUV, and a small BMW sports car. He drove around the driveway, which circled back around to the entrance, and parked.

"I'll be right back, stay here," he said. I nodded and leaned against the bike.

"And don't talk to anyone," he called back as he walked up to the large marble steps. I stuck my tongue out and he smiled and ran inside.

A few minutes later he came out and got on the bike. A girl with long black hair and olive skin like Jag ran to the doorway after him. She was dressed in a private school uniform and looked distraught.

"No, Jason, wait!" she called, running down the marble steps.

"Jason?" I breathed, confused.

"Come on," he said, angrily revving the engine before speeding away.

He didn't tell me what that was about until we got back to his trailer. Even then, he made me wait until we were out back on the small porch, a cigarette lit and half smoked, before he spoke.

"That's my parents' house," he started with, taking a long drag. "My mom gives me money every few months so I can live on my own since my dad kicked me out about two years ago," he inhaled on the end of his cigarette, hard, and looked at the deck below us. The wood was rotting—if you nudged it hard enough with your foot I'm sure it would give. He took another long drag and sighed, running his fingers through his hair.

"I couldn't go earlier because I got detention, which made me get out late, and my Dad was there when I went to go earlier before I got you, so I had to go after, and yeah," he sighed, rambling as he fumbled with his pack for another smoke.

"And that girl?"

"Juliet, my sister, she's 14,"

"And why did she call you Jason?" I asked hesitantly. I leaned back against the wooden railing and crossed my arms slowly.

"That's my Dad's family name, he gave it to his son, and the day he told me he never thought of me as his son I changed my name. My middle name is Augustin, and my nickname as a kid was Jagger—Jag, so I just changed it, moved out, and that's how things are," he inhaled another long, shaky drag.

"So, I guess meeting your parents is out of the question," I said. He laughed a short laugh and sighed. He put his cigarette out and looked at me.

"You know, I've never told anyone this." I nodded and walked over and sat in his lap and hugged him.

"Thank you for telling me," I said into the crook of his neck. He hugged me back, slowly and hesitantly.

"I think I'm in love with you," I breathed. He was silent for a long time so I sat up and looked at him. He had a half smile on his face.

"What? I said, standing.

"Nothing," he smiled.

"Tell me," I leaned against the porch rail a few feet away. He stood and put his hands on either side of me.

"I know I love you," he breathed before kissing me. I couldn't help but smile. I wrapped my arms around him and kissed him, curving my body into his. He moved his hands from the porch to my hips, his thumbs grazing my bare midriff. Suddenly, it started to downpour snow and sleet at the same time. We ran inside, soaking wet and shivering.

"Here, you can take a hot shower and borrow clothes. Your lips are blue," he said, a chuckle on the last part. I nodded, a violent shiver ripped through my body. He started to get nervous, "Come on, I'll get the water on, undress," he went over to the small bathroom, pulling the curtain aside and turned the water on hot. I undressed to my soaked through bra and panties and he turned and stopped.

"I love New England weather," he sighed happily. I laughed, my teeth chattering a bit and walked over.

"The hot water runs out about 5 to 10 minutes in," he said as I closed the curtain.

"What about you, aren't you freezing?" I poked my head out from behind the curtain.

"I'll live," he said pulling his shirt over his head and undoing his jeans, kicking them off.

I showered for a few minutes and once I was warm I stepped out and dried myself with the towel hanging over the curtain.

"Do you have clothes I can borrow?" I asked, wringing my hair out in the shower floor.

"Yeah, here." He called from the other room.

I wrapped the towel around my body and pushed the curtain aside. He dropped the shirt that was in his hands and looked me up and down.

"What?" I laughed, walking over.

"Nothing," he mumbled, chuckling softly. He handed me a pair of boxer briefs, sweats, and a thick long-sleeved shirt. I pulled the briefs on under the towel then the shirt on over it and pulled the towel out then pulled the sweats on. He pouted slightly that he didn't get to see anything and I laughed.

"Even though we might be in love I'm still not sleeping with you. Yet," I said, putting my hand on his bare chest and pushed him back playfully. I sat cross legged on his bed, drying my hair with the towel, and he walked over in just sweat pants and fell onto his side next to me. I got under the covers and shivered.

"Crap. I should bring my bike in," he said, getting up and pulling on boots before running outside with no shirt on. I sat up and he pushed the bike inside and wiped it off with a towel. I laughed and smiled at the sight, pulling my knees to my chest, hugging them with my arms. He glanced over at me, smiled, then went back to what he was doing.

After he was done with his bike, he locked the door and opened the window that was in the bedroom. There was already at least half a foot of snow and ice on the ground. My phone rang and I crawled over to my bag and looked at the caller ID, it was Dani.

"I'm at Mason's can you cover for me?"

"I'm at Jag's." I laughed.

"Crap, what do we do?" She giggled. My phone beeped. I was getting another call, Dad.

"Dad's calling me, I'll figure something out," I said, hanging up on her.

"Hey, Dad," I said, trying to calm the nervous tone that was quavering through my voice.

"Carter, glad I caught you. Power and service lines are going down everywhere, they're saying this is the worst storm yet. I'm stuck at the hospital, won't be back till noon, maybe later. Are you and your sister home?"

"Yeah," I lied casually.

"Good, stay safe."

"You too, Dad," I said bye and hung up and Jag was back in bed. I got back under the covers and wrapped my arms around his bare stomach.

"My Dad said power lines are going down everywhere," I rested my head on his chest.

"Well if people are losing power then the trailer park will be the first to go," he said simply.

"We can keep each other warm," I mused, kissing him softly.

We started to watch TV and kiss occasionally. A few minutes later the TV cut and the power went out. He sighed and stood.

"I have some candles in here somewhere for shit like this," he said, opening a cabinet and grabbing a few thick, white candles. He whipped out his lighter and lit the candles and placed them around the bedroom. We talked and joked around until falling asleep to each other's laughter.

When I woke up the next morning I smiled at Jag, who was still asleep next to me. I got up and peeked behind the curtain, the snow was coming up to the trailer's window and still falling. I jumped on Jag and playfully shook his shoulders.

"We're going to be trapped!" I laughed, he smiled and rubbed his eyes.

"I'm okay with it," he yawned, holding me close.

"No, really Jag, look outside!" He stood and pulled the window curtain all the way open.

"Shit," he said, looking out at all the snow. He looked at me and we laughed, and he sat back and lit a cigarette. I sat on the bed and cuddled up against his side.

"So, will you not have sex with me because you're a virgin?" He said softly, completely out of nowhere.

"No," I said after a few minutes of silence. "Are you?"

"No," a hint of pride was in his voice. I sat on the bed with him and laid down on my back. He looked down at me and kissed me then sat back up.

"So, have you ever been in a relationship like this?"

He shook his head, stroking my cheek, "I've never met anyone like you, and I think that's why." He kissed me softly.

"Why am I special?"

"Because, you're not all preppy and girly like the other girls and you get me. You don't whine and beg me to share my feelings or tell you what I'm thinking. You're independent and don't pry, especially when I had to bring you to my old house. And your just so easy to love, you know, when you're not screaming or kicking doors off your truck at me," he said, a smile on his face when he said the last part.

"I can't help that my truck is really old!" I laughed.

"Or you're just freakishly strong," he joked. I laughed and shoved his bare chest. He laughed and leaned over me and kissed me, wrapping his arms around me. I smiled and snuggled into his chest. This was my happy place.

Chapter Eleven

Jagger

Around 3 P.M. the snow finally stopped and we got dressed. She pulled my shirt over her head and hooked her bra before pulling her jeans on. Her shirt was still wet so she stuffed it in her bag and pulled back on the shirt I lent her.

"Come on, let's go shovel a path out," she said. I pulled on a sweatshirt and my leather jacket and handed her a sweatshirt. She pulled it on then pulled on her jacket and I opened the door. We pushed the snow off my steps and the rest was plowed earlier so I walked towards her truck.

"Come on," I said to Carter. She was standing with her back to me, leaning against the banister. She turned and I was hit in the face with a snowball.

"Oh, so that's how it is," I laughed, grabbing up a handful of snow. She laughed and shrieked as I hit her in the back with a snowball. We pelted snowballs at each other till we were both out of breath and laughing hysterically.

Finally, we got in her truck and drove to her house.

"Do you want to come in?" she said as I walked her to the door.

"Um," I said looking for her Dad's car.

"He's not here," she laughed unlocking the door.

"I guess I could come in for a little," I said walking in after her. She climbed a staircase to a lofted room. She had a bed on the far wall, a room separator, a desk littered with papers and photos, an open closet, a small sofa, a TV on a chest at the end of the bed. She grabbed a fancy, expensive looking camera and pointed it at me.

"Smile," she sang, flashing the camera. She looked at it and laughed.

"I don't photograph well," I said walking over.

"Oh yeah?" she laughed.

"Yeah," I nodded wrapped my arms around her waist. She put her face to mine and took a photo then looked at it. Stupid grins and goofy eyes covered our faces.

"Let's try again," she giggled, setting up the camera. I looked at her gorgeous smile and kissed her. The photo snapped and she blushed and looked at the camera. It was a perfect photo. She put the camera on her desk and wrapped her arms around my neck. I slid my hands on her waist and kissed her. We kissed for a while before we heard a door slam and her dad called her name.

"Go down to the garage," she said. I nodded and kissed her one last time before going down the staircase and walked down the driveway. I walked into town and went to Frank's bar and got a beer.

A few hours later I was sitting at the bar when the door opened. I turned and did a double take. My dad walked in and sat down two stools away from me.

"You know your serving a minor, right?" he said to Frank, who was currently behind the bar drying glasses.

"Eh, no one is around, and the kid, Jag," He nodded his chin at me, "He's like my son," he said, smiling at me. I nodded back and finished my beer.

"After you kicked me out, Frank let me stay in the back room till I got a place of my own," I said, putting some money down on the bar.

"Thanks, Frank, I'll see you later."

He nodded and saluted me with two fingers.

"Jason, wait," He called out after me.

"That's not my name anymore." I didn't turn around.

"Fine, Jag, can we talk please?" He said, I could hear the bar stool scrape against the linoleum floor as he stood.

"No."

And with that, I walked out. He ran out after me, stopped, and watched as I walked away.

"I'll give you immediate access to the first million of your inheritance if you come home, and the rest of it if you stay, at least until you graduate, your mother and Juliet miss you," he said. I stopped and bit my lip, a million alone would solve a lot. It would solve everything, really. Except it was Jason Sr., and with him there were always strings attached.

"On what condition?" I asked, my back still to him.

"You just have to come home. No strings, Jagger, your mother and sister miss you, and I know you won't come just because I ask nicely," he said. I laughed and sighed, looking down.

"I need to think about it," I said, still not turning to look at him.

"Okay, well, stop by any time," he said slowly. I sighed and walked off.

I was lying in bed that night thinking about the offer. I couldn't sleep; I needed to talk to Carter. I looked at the clock on the stove, 11:30 P.M. She'd still be up. I pulled on jeans and a t-shirt and grabbed my jacket before hoping on my bike and riding to her house. There was a light on in one of her windows so I jumped on the lower balcony and grabbed the floor of her balcony and pulled myself up. I climbed over the rail and looked in her window. She was sitting on her bed in underwear and a tank top rubbing lotion on her legs. I tapped on the window and she turned and smiled, running over.

"What are you doing here?" she laughed quietly, opening the window.

"I needed to talk to you about something," I said, climbing in.

"What's up?" she wiped her hands on a towel.

"Today I was at Frank's bar and my father comes in, offers me immediate access to the first million of my inheritance to come home, and then the rest of it if I stay until I graduate," I said slowly after a long time of silence.

"Holy crap."

"Yeah," I nodded.

"Well, are you going to do it?" she asked, sitting cross-legged on the end of her bed. "I don't know," I sighed, leaning against her desk.

"What's holding you back?"

"Having to live with my dad, and his rules. Especially after everything that has happened, and been said, you know?"

"And what's making you want to go?"

"The money, not having to pay rent, getting to see Juliet more than once every few months. She needs some protection from our fucked up lives, and I won't have to be there after I graduate if I don't want to, so I guess it's stupid easy money," I sighed, running my fingers through my hair.

"Well it looks like you just answered your own question," she smiled, walking over and leaned against me.

"I guess," I sighed.

"I'm going to miss that trailer," she said softly into my chest. I laughed and kissed her.

"You'll like the estate better, it's got heating and plumbing that actually works." She smiled and kissed me.

"Now go, before my dad catches you," she smiled, shooing me down the stairs.

"By the way, can I borrow your truck to move back in tomorrow?" I laughed, looking up at her from the bottom of the stairs.

"I'll be over at 8," she smiled, blowing me a kiss.

The next morning Carter helped me pack everything up and load it onto her truck bed; then she drove the truck and I drove my motorcycle over to the estate. My mom was already waiting outside to greet us.

"Mom, this is Carter. Carter, this is Trina, my mom" I said, the last part hesitantly.

"It's so nice to meet you," she gushed.

"You, too," Carter smiled.

"The staff can move everything in. I kept your room just the way you left it, now come sit, let's talk," she said pulling us inside. Once the question and answer was over and everything was moved in, I gave Carter a tour of the estate. I ended it with my room, going up to the double doors and turning to look at her. She smiled and I kissed her cheek and then turned.

"And this is my room," I said as I opened the double doors.

"Wow this place is like, five times the size of your trailer," she laughed looking around. I sighed and shrugged, walking out to the balcony so I could light a cigarette.

Carter and I were sitting on the balcony talking when the doors opened.

"It's true!" Juliet cried, running in and hugging me.

"Yeah," I said taking a drag.

"And you must be the girl," she looked at Carter.

"Carter, my sister Juliet," I said motioning to them.

"Hi," Carter smiled shaking her hand.

"It's so nice to meet you and you're so pretty," Juliet gushed. Carter blushed and smiled at her.

"Juliet, I'll see you at dinner. Can we have some time?" I said. She nodded and smiled, kissed my cheek, and all but skipped out. I closed the door behind her and walked inside.

"If I remember correctly this bed is a lot more comfortable than my mattress back in the trailer," I said, sitting on the edge of the king-sized bed.

"Oh, is it now, or is that just a ploy to get me into bed?" she laughed, walking over to me slowly. I smiled and pulled her in between my legs and kissed her.

"Both," I admitted.

She laughed and jumped on the bed and pulled me on top of her. I pulled my jacket off and threw it on the ground and she held me closer. She started to kiss my neck and ear and I bit my lip. She slid her hand down my chest and started to unbutton my shirt. She moved so she was on my lap and I pushed her shirt over her head and pulled her down to kiss me again. I slid my hands down her bare back until I reached her hips. She kissed me more passionately and I gripped her closer to me. There was a quiet knock on the door and my dad poked his head in then stepped out when he saw us.

"Sorry," he called.

"Hang on," I said to Carter, groaning as I walked out of the room. I opened the door, my father was standing in the wide hallway, tugging on the cuffs of his dress shirt uncomfortably.

"What?" I said, buttoning my jeans and closing the door behind me.

"Glad you came back," he said tightly, handing me an envelope. I peeked in it and saw a check, smiling to myself I shoved it in my back pocket and laughed.

"You're not glad I came back, you're glad you got your way and Trina off your back," I smirked.

He straightened his ever-present tie and brushed some lint off his black suit jacket, "In regards to your inheritance, you will gain access to it on your 18th birthday instead of your 25th, as it would have normally been."

"Sounds fine to me."

"Who's that?" He asked nodding towards the door.

"No one that concerns you. Now the only way I'm staying here is if we don't talk, you don't talk to that girl, you don't control me in any way, that girl and I come and go as we please, and you don't try and parent me in any way, got it?" I said. He sighed and nodded slowly.

"I do regret what I said that night, very much so," he said slowly.

"Don't bother," I scoffed, going back inside.

Chapter Twelve

Jagger

I was at the auto shop after school working on Carter's truck when she walked in, leaning against the side of it.

"What again are you working on today?" she asked, wiping some grease off my cheek with her thumb. I smiled and looked at her, I could only see the bottom of her face with how the hood was propped. I ducked out from under it and kissed her nose.

"Today is your transmission," I said. I had decided to slowly rebuild the engine now that I had some money to burn.

"I thought that was last week," she said, her hands on my sides.

"No, I got the new one in last week. I'm putting it in now," I said, wiping my hands on a rag so I didn't get grease on her clothes. "I can't have your truck breaking down or falling apart. I need you to be safe," I said. She grinned at the sentiment and kissed me.

"My hero," she fake swooned. I laughed and tucked the rag back into my pocket.

"I should have this finished up by tonight. I can drop it off at your house when I'm done," I said, looking at the engine.

"I need to do some homework at the library anyways, so I can hang around until you're finished," she said, grabbing her backpack out of the cab. "Just text me when you're all set," she said, kissing my cheek. I smiled and nodded.

"Love you," I called after her as she walked out.

"Well aren't you just one smitten kitten?" Kent said as he walked over. I shoved him and he laughed.

"What do you have planned for Valentine's?" he asked, sitting on a stool nearby.

"Valentine's?"

"Yes, dumbass, its next week," he laughed.

"Uh, I don't know," I shrugged, ducking back under the hood.

"Dude, you've been together what, five months now? You know she's going to be expecting something," he said. I sighed, ducking back out from the hood.

"You know, for once you might be right," I sighed, scratching the back of my head. He laughed and swiveled on the stool.

"I know," he smirked.

"I better plan something," I sighed before getting back to work.

Later that night I was at Carter's house watching a movie with her when she went to go make some popcorn. The front door opened and Dani came in, dropping her backpack loudly on the floor.

"Hey, Jagger," she called, about to head upstairs.

"Dani, wait, come over here," I said quietly, hoping Carter didn't hear. She looked at me, confused, then it turned to intrigue and she waltzed over.

"Yes?" she asked, sitting on the back on the couch.

"Valentine's is coming up and I have no idea what to do," I whispered. She laughed and patted my head.

"Oh, Jag," she mused. I frowned at her and she sighed, removing her hand.

"She hasn't been to Boston once since we've been here, maybe take her there?" she shrugged, standing and smoothing her skirt.

"That's actually not a bad idea, thanks," I nodded, and she smiled and walked off.

"I'm smarter than I look," she sang as she went up the stairs. I laughed and sat back, the plans already forming in my mind.

Valentine's was on a Friday this year, which was perfect. I told Carter we were going to dinner, and

I had Dani pack an overnight bag when Carter wasn't home, stashing it in the truck before school. We left right after classes and once I had driven two towns out, Carter began to realize something was up.

"Where are we going to dinner?" she asked, confused as I got onto the highway.

"It's a surprise," I smiled, winking at her. She laughed and shoved me playfully and I grabbed her hand when she did, bringing it to my lips and kissed each knuckle. She blushed and looked out the window.

An hour later she saw the exit sign for Boston and turned to me, eyes wide with excitement, a huge smile on her face.

"Boston?!" she asked. I smiled and nodded. She threw her arms around me, kissing my cheek. I smiled and pulled her close to me on the bench seat and held her tight as I drove to the hotel in the heart of the city.

"I didn't bring any overnight things," she said, eyes wide. I smiled and squeezed her.

"I had Dani pack a bag for you," I smiled and she laughed.

"You are amazing," she mused, kissing my cheek again. We got out at the hotel and a valet took the truck. I grabbed her bag and my bag out of the bed before he drove off and we walked into the lobby. Her eyes went wide at the lavish décor and I smiled, content with how the plans had gone thus far. We checked in and went up to our room, and when I opened the door she ran in to scope it out. I smiled and followed her, closing the door behind me and dropping our bags by the closet. To the left was the bathroom and past that was the room, a large space with high ceilings. There was a king bed against the wall to my left, a large TV mounted on the wall across from it, a small seating area was off by the windows, and a desk was to the left of the TV. Carter had opened the curtains, exposing a breathtaking view of Boston and the Charles River.

"Jason Hastings, you have outdone yourself," she said, still facing the windows. I smiled and walked up behind her, wrapping my arms around her shoulders.

"This is just the beginning," I whispered in her ear before kissing it. She turned and hugged me tight, her face against my chest.

"Oh how I love you so much," she said. I smiled and kissed the top of her head.

"Feeling's mutual," I smiled, holding her tight.

After she explored the rest of the hotel room—opening all the cabinets and smelling all the products in the bathroom—she grabbed her bag off the floor and put it on the end of the bed. She opened it and laughed, pulling out a dress I had never seen before. It was a soft, rosy pink little thing with a low-cut neck line and off the shoulder sleeves. She laid it out on the bed and dug through the rest of her bag.

"I am going to kill that little bitch," she laughed, throwing her hands up. Her cheeks were hot with anger.

"What? Why?" I asked, confused. I sat up from my spot at the head of the bed and looked over.

"All Dani packed me was this dress—which is hers, heels—also hers, and lingerie!" she laughed, pulling a handful of colorful lingerie out of the bag. I laughed so hard I fell back on the bed. "What are you laughing at?!" she cried, throwing the handful of underwear at me. I propped myself up on my elbows and looked at her.

"I told her to pack you something nice for dinner and then something to sleep in for the hotel, I didn't know she would do this," I said, breaking out into another fit of laughter. Carter pulled her phone out of her pocket and dialed Dani, putting it on speaker.

"Hello?" Dani's voice called out.

"You dumb slut, did you think what you packed me is a joke?" Carter snapped, pacing the length of the room. Dani's laughter echoed out of the phone and I laughed too.

"Did Jag laugh? I thought it was funny!" she joked.

"Dani!" Carter groaned.

"Carter that dress will look amazing on you and you'll thank me later for the other stuff," Dani said, her voice condescending.

"Oh yeah, I'll thank you later," Carter shot back, hanging up on her. She looked at me and I shrugged my shoulders.

"That dress will look amazing on you," I offered. She shot me a look then went into the bathroom, snatching up the dress on her way.

I had changed into my suit by the time she came out of the bathroom wearing the dress. I was right, she did look amazing. The neckline showed off her petite shoulders and delicate collar bones. She smoothed the skirt down, which ended about mid-thigh, and looked at me.

"Well?" she asked.

"I'm at a loss for words," I smiled, taking her hand in mine and twirling her. She laughed and shoved me and then grabbed the heels off the bed.

"You look handsome, I don't think I've ever seen you in a suit," she said, giving me a once over.

"You haven't," I joked, trying to tie my tie. She smiled and walked over, untying the messy knot I had made and tied it for me perfectly.

"My Dad can't tie one for the life of him," she said, straightening the knot and fixing my collar. I smiled and kissed her forehead.

"Ready?" I asked, offering her my hand. She grabbed her leather jacket and nodded, taking my hand in hers. We walked to the restaurant, a small, intimate, old school Italian bistro tucked away on a side street.

After an amazing meal, we left the restaurant and Carter went to walk in the direction of the hotel. I pulled her the opposite direction and she looked at me, an intrigued look on her perfect face.

"What else do you have up your sleeve, Hastings?" she asked and I smiled and wrapped my arm around her, pulling her the opposite way. I led her to the Museum of Fine Arts and stopped in front of it.

"That's sweet, Jag, but I think it closed like an hour ago," she said, kissing my cheek.

"Let's just check it out," I urged, pulling her towards the door.

"Jason Hastings, if you think I am breaking and entering you are mental," she said as I rattled the doorknob. I looked at her, giving her a mischievous grin before knocking on the door. She looked at me, confused and slightly irritated, then the door opened.

"Mr. Hastings, welcome," the curator smiled, opening the door wider. I shook his hand and pulled a dumbstruck Carter through the doors.

"Jag, what the hell is going on?" Carter whispered.

"I got you a museum," I smiled, waving my arms around. Her jaw dropped and I laughed, looking at the curator, who smiled. "Well, at least for the next two hours I got you a museum," I smirked. She smacked me with her purse and I laughed, pulling her into my arms.

"You are insane!" she gushed, looking around like a kid in a candy shop. I smiled and nodded at the curator, who nodded back then headed to his office.

"Happy Valentine's Day," I said as she looked around, eyes still wide. She looked at me completely awestruck.

"You are the most amazing boyfriend in the entire world," she laughed, running over and jumping into my arms. I smiled and twirled her around.

"Now go, nerd out over art," I smiled, motioning for her to lead the way.

Chapter Thirteen

Carter

I woke up and stretched, smacking Jag in the face by accident. He blinked, a confused and stunned look on his previously peaceful face. He looked at me, a small red mark on his forehead from where my knuckles had collided with him. I giggled and kissed him.

"I'm so sorry," I laughed, "I guess I'm still not used to sleeping in a bed with someone," I admitted. He smiled and caressed my cheek, still half asleep.

"It's okay babe, it's only been a few months," he mumbled, starting to doze off.

"Jag, it's been 6 months," I whispered in his ear before kissing him.

"Oh shit dude, you're right," he laughed, pulling me into his arms. "Happy anniversary," he said, hugging me tight.

"Happy anniversary, love," I smiled, cuddling into him. I looked at the clock on his bedside table and groaned. "I know it's our anniversary but I have to leave soon if I'm going to make it to the Art Institute on time," I sighed, squeezing his forearm. He groaned, pulling me closer.

"No, don't go," he mused, kissing my neck and ear. I turned and kissed him then sat up.

"I'm sorry Jag, its accepted student's day and I really want to see the campus," I said, moving his thick, muscular arm off my lap. He nodded, rolling over and pulling a pillow to his chest.

"Drive safe, love you," he mumbled before falling back asleep. I smiled and pulled his shirt that I slept in when I stayed here over my head and got dressed. I grabbed my bag and closed the door quietly. I was opening the front door when I heard someone clear their throat behind me. Mr. Hastings was standing in the foyer dressed in a sharp suit, a sleek leather brief case in his hand.

"Good morning, Ms. Baker," he nodded curtly. I smiled a tight smile.

"Mr. Hastings," I said softly.

"Where are you headed to this early on a Saturday?" he asked, straightening his tie. I noticed during the few months that Jag had been back living in his family's estate this was one of his father's nervous ticks.

"I have accepted student's day, the school is in New York so I need to get an early start," I said, tugging on the hem of my sweater.

"Glad to see you're planning on attending a college, I wish Jag had the same collegiate initiative," He said, extending his arm to look at his shiny gold Rolex. "Well, we both better get going then," he said, motioning to the door. I nodded and we walked out. I headed over to my truck and he headed over to the three-car garage. I drove away before I could see what expensive, gaudy car he would drive out in.

After three hours, I got to the Art Institute. A huge banner welcomed accepted students and I smiled and took a photo of it. I walked around campus then went to the function room where the first event was being held. After a long introduction from the Dean of Students we were to group off by prospective major for the rest of the day's activities. I walked over to the photography booth and mingled with a bunch of the other students there.

"I've been dying to get the new Nikon, though," I said to a girl I had been talking to. A tall guy popped over and smiled, "Sorry to interject, but I actually just got the new Nikon, it's amazing," he said, smiling a dazzling smile. I looked at him, he was tall, at least a full foot taller than me, dark blue eyes, his dirty blond hair was messily coiffed and he was slender but muscular.

"Really? I'm so jealous, I have been drooling over it since it came out! I mean the shutter speed alone!" I laughed. He smiled and nodded, taking out his phone.

"It truly is worth all the hype, let me show you some photos I took of this bird, I was hiking and I caught it swooping in to get a fish from a lake, snapping it, and flying off. It was unreal," he said, showing me some amazing photos.

"That's epic, I mean the picture quality is out of this world," I said, holding his hand to pull his phone closer. "These are amazing, do you have more?" I said, looking up at him. He smiled down at me, a little wide eyed, then shook his head a bit and nodded.

"Uh, yeah, a bunch more from that hike on here, then I keep my portfolio in my car, I could show it to you after this, if you'd like," he said. I smiled and nodded.

"I would love that!" I grinned, then motioned for him to show me more photos. He happily obliged.

"I'm Alex, by the way," he said, offering me his hand.

"Carter," I smiled, shaking it.

Alex and I stuck together for the rest of the day. We had tours of the dorms, the classroom buildings, the campus, and the student union. We also had lunch, played some run of the mill icebreakers, then we were all left to our own devices to explore the area. A bunch of us from the photography group had bonded pretty well and decided to check out a couple of the local galleries. I was staring at a painting when Alex walked up next to me.

"We're all gonna head back to campus, it's getting pretty late, and a few of us have some long drives home. You coming with?" he said, nudging me. I nodded and smiled.

"Lead the way," I said. As we were walking back to campus I looked up at him. "How bad is your drive?" I asked, swinging my bag back and forth.

"Not crazy bad, I live in southern Vermont, so about five to six hours," he said. I let out a whistle.

"I thought my drive back to Massachusetts was bad," I laughed. He shrugged and smiled, hands in his pockets.

"Hey, want to see my portfolio?" he asked once we were back in the parking garage.

"Of course!" I smiled, nodding. We walked over to a Jeep Wrangler and he unlocked it, and grabbed a black leather portfolio case from his back seat. We sat on a low concrete wall and he took out his photos and I flipped through them.

"These are amazing, the detail, the color, they're all so vivid," I smiled up at him. He looked at me, his eyes searching. Was he going to kiss me? Oh, God, I need to stop this. He even started to lean over. "Uh, Alex, I have a boyfriend," I said softly. He stopped in his tracks and straightened up.

"Right, sorry, caught up in the moment." He said, moving so he was sitting fully straight, even moving a few inches away from me.

"Yo, Alex!" someone called. He looked around. A tall guy, probably the same absurd height as Alex walked over. He had shaggy, strawberry blond hair, bright blue eyes, a handsome face, with a muscular build and broad shoulders. "I've been looking for you everywhere."

"Pat, hey," Alex said, standing up. I stood and wiped off the butt of my jeans. I straightened Alex's photos and put them back in his portfolio. I handed them to him and he tucked it under his arm. "Pat, this is Carter, she's an incoming student here too," Alex said. "Carter, this is my friend Pat, he's going here for drawing." I smiled and shook his hand.

"Nice to meet you," I smiled. He nodded, his blue eyes searching mine.

"Pleasure is all mine," he smiled.

"Well, we should get going," Alex said, slapping Pat on the back. Pat nodded, and they both looked at me. I smiled and waved.

"It was nice meeting you guys," I said, tucking a piece of hair behind my ear.

"You too," they both said, then looked at each other. They got in Alex's car and I waved as they drove off. I shook my head and walked to my truck, getting in. Weirdest day ever.

I drove back home and parked. I sat in the car for a long time, taking in the day. I sighed, getting out of the truck and closing the door. I leaned against it, putting my head to the cool glass window. I exhaled, stood up, and walked inside. I opened my bedroom door and stopped in my tracks. The entire room was filled with sunflowers. I laughed, dropping my bag on the floor and walked in. There was a large white envelope on my desk. I picked it up, it was thick cardstock, "Carter" scrawled on the front in Jag's handwriting. I opened it and slipped out the card. It was a simple piece of white card stock with "I love you, I love you, I love you!" scrawled on it. I smiled and hugged it to my chest.

"He spent all day setting it up," I heard my Dad say. I turned, he was standing in my doorway. I smiled and leaned against my desk. "Kid shows up around 9 A.M. with a whole damn van of flowers, asking me if he can come in," he laughed, crossing his arms. I smiled, the whole room was filled with yellow—with happiness and love.

"You look happy, Carter," he said, walking in, putting his hands on my shoulders. I smiled and nodded.

"I am, Dad, so unbelievably happy," I said. He smiled and squeezed my shoulders.

"Good, I'm glad," he said, kissing my forehead before walking out. He wasn't big on displays of affection, so that was big for us. I smiled and sat on my bed and called Jag.

"You are crazy," I laughed, picking up some of the flowers. He chuckled and I smiled, I couldn't stop smiling.

"Crazy in love," he said. I laughed at how cliché he could be some times.

"This is amazing, Jason, thank you," I said. I knew he hated when I used his full name, so I only did it when I wanted him to know I was serious.

"No, Car, thank you, for being you, and doing all you do for me," he said. "I have to go, I picked up a shift at the bar, but I'll see you tomorrow," he said.

"Tomorrow," I agreed before hanging up.

Chapter Fourteen

Carter

We'd been dating for about nine months now and Jag and I were sitting on his balcony kissing on the giant outside couch. We parted and he looked at me and stroked my cheek.

"I'd never thought I'd be able to feel this way about someone before," he admitted.

"Me either," I said softly, kissing him.

"So, you excited for graduation?" I asked. He shrugged and kissed me.

"How about you?" I nodded and smiled.

"We're going out after, right?" he said. I nodded and kissed him again.

"What are you going to do this summer?" I asked.

"Frank offered me a full time job at the bar, but, I don't know," he laughed, "What do you want to do?" he smiled, stroking my cheek.

"I've always wanted to travel the world before college but I could never afford it."

"I can afford it. Want to travel the world with me?" he asked simply.

I sat up and looked at him, he was lying on the couch still, smiling up at me with dumbstruck eyes, a small, playful smile on his lips.

"Don't joke about that," I said. He smiled and sat up, taking my hands in his.

"I'm not, why don't we? I have money and a girl I love who has a dream, why not make it happen?" he said, rather matter-o-fact. He brought my hands up to his lips and kissed each one softly.

"Oh my God, you're kidding me," I laughed and putting my hand on his chest.

"I'm not joking, I would love to travel the world with you," he smiled.

"I couldn't," I sighed, shaking my head slowly, the reality of the gesture sinking in.

"Think about it as a graduation present," he smiled.

"You're amazing," I laughed, hugging him. He smiled and kissed me, pulling me back down on the couch on top of him, wrapping his arms around me.

"We can leave a week after graduation, I'll have the family travel agent schedule everything, just give me a list of places you want to go," he said, stroking my cheek.

"This is too amazing," I laughed. He smiled and kissed me.

"I love you," I said.

"I love you, too," he smiled.

The next day I woke up, showered, and dried my hair. "Can I do your hair?" Dani asked, walked in wearing a tank top and a pair of boxer shorts.

"Sure," I pulled a stool into the bathroom. She curled my hair into long perfect curls and tousled my bangs.

"Let me see your dress," she said. I held up a yellow sun dress with a halter neck that ended at my mid-thigh.

"Pretty," she smiled.

"So, how's Jag?" she asked as I went behind my room separator to change into my strapless lace underwear.

"Good, guess what he's giving me for graduation," I said, walking out in my underwear.

"Ooh someone's having some fun tonight! She laughed, clapping her hands, "I don't know, tell me," she smiled, crossing her arms.

"He's taking me on a trip around the world before college, like I've always wanted," I smiled, moisturizing my legs.

"Oh my God; that's amazing," she smiled.

"Yeah," I laughed. I nodded and slipped on my dress.

"You look good," she said.

"Thanks," I smiled, looking at myself in the mirror.

"I really like this new medicine you're on," she said, coming up behind me and fixing my hair.

"Me, too," I smiled, and we both shared a small, knowing laugh together. I sat on the end of my bed and slipped on my heels. I folded the bag with my cap and gown in it over my arm and grabbed my phone.

"Take photos," I said, handing her my camera. She nodded and slid it over her neck.

"So, what are you going to do about college and Jag?"

"I don't know, we'll figure it out as we go," I shrugged. She nodded and stood. I heard Jag's motorcycle outside and I quickly did my make-up before looking at Dani.

"You look great, Car," she said. I smiled and went down through the garage staircase and walked outside.

"Damn," he said getting off his bike. He was wearing clean jeans and a crisp, white button down.

"I'll take that as a compliment," I smiled, kissing him. "Ready to graduate?"

"As ready as I'll ever be," he smiled.

The next morning, I woke up and he wasn't in bed. I pulled on one of his t-shirts and a pair of jeans I left from God only knows when and checked the balcony, nothing. I went down the stairs slowly. He was sitting at the dining room table with a man in a suit.

"Hey, Carter this is the family's travel agent, Louis. Lou, this is my girlfriend, Carter," he said getting up.

"Hey," I smiled pushing the sleeves back.

"We're just going over the final plans for our trip," he said.

"Oh, okay," I smiled. "You'll get to spend about a week in each place, and you'll be able to go to about six or eight places," he said taking out a map, red X's on all the places I wanted to go.

"This is perfect," I smiled.

"Now, I have you booked at all the best hotels and first class for flying, or the overnight train cars when taking trains," he said.

"Thank you for this," I said kissing Jag's check. He smiled and squeezed my hand. Lou smiled and put everything in a folder.

"Here you go, all your tickets and information are in there, have a great trip," he said. Jag nodded and shook his hand.

"Thanks, Lou," he said. Lou nodded and left.

"I'm so excited," I said. Jag smiled and we went upstairs. He went out on the balcony and lit a cigarette.

"You have no idea how much you have changed my life over the past nine months," he said, looking at me. I was sitting on the couch cross legged, the folder open in my lap. I looked up and smiled then I stuck my tongue out at him and he laughed, "I'm being serious, Car." He urged. "Really, I used to be a no-good asshole who only smoked and drank and skipped classes and now I have a reason to be nice, to be a good person" he said. I smiled and hugged him.

"I love you," I said into his shoulder.

"I love you too," he said. I smiled and sighed. I had never been happier.

Chapter Fifteen

Carter

A week later we were on a plane to France, after that we were going to go to Italy, Spain, Ireland, Greece, and Egypt.

"So, you excited for school?" He asked as we were getting off our plane in Paris.

"Yes, I can't wait to go to college," I laughed as we dragged our giant duffels to the car waiting for us. We got in the back seat and he smiled at me.

"We should talk about that, college, me leaving."

"Let's just enjoy our trip, we can talk after," he smiled. I nodded and sat back, his hand in mine.

Two months later, we were on our way back to the states, and finally in the car back home when I looked at Jag.

"We've been avoiding this topic for nearly three months now, what are we going to do when I go to school?" I said slowly.

"What do you mean?" he asked, looking at me, a cigarette hanging between his lips.

"When I go to school, what are we going to do about our relationship? I'll be in New York and you'll be back in Boston, that's far," I said taking his hand in mine.

"Yeah and?" he said looking more confused.

"I don't know, I'll be in college, you'll be working in the bar, shit can happen. I just want to know what we're going to do about us," I said looking down then back at him. He put his cigarette out and looked at me.

"Are we breaking up?" he said confused.

"Not unless you think that's what's best for us," I said slowly.

"Well I don't want to," he said.

"Me either," I said.

"Then we stay together, I can ride my bike down and visit you and we can make it work," he said. I nodded and kissed him.

"I love you," I said hugging him close.

"Love you too, Car," he said holding my back. The car pulled up to my house and we got out and he carried my bag to the door.

"See you when we bring your stuff up," he said. I nodded and wrapped my arms around his neck and kissed him.

"Thank you, for everything," I said. He smiled and kissed me. I hugged him closer and then stepped back.

"See you in a couple days," I said. He nodded and got back in the car.

It was finally move in day, Dani and I finished packing up my truck with enough room for Jag's bike to fit in the back for him to ride back on, when Jag pulled up.

"Hey Carter, Dani," He said walking over to kiss me.

"Hey, Jag," Dani said. I smiled and kissed him back.

"So, I'm taking you back with me?" he said. She nodded and threw her purse in the cab of the truck before getting in.

"Ready to go to college?" Jag said, his hands on my hips.

"Yeah," I said wrapping my arms around his neck. Dani blew the horn and yelled for us to hurry up. Jag sighed and slid the plank of wood we kept in the bed of my truck out and created a ramp, we led his bike up it and secured it in the cab. He got in and I closed my door and drove off. Three hours later, I pulled into my dorm at the Art Institute and we brought my bags and boxes up to my room. My roommate wasn't here yet so we unpacked and set everything up. Once we were done, Jag unloaded his bike and looked at me.

"I love you," he said kissing me.

"I love you too," I said hugging him close.

"Love 'ya, Sis," I smiled, giving her an awkward half hug.

"You too," she smiled.

"I'll be back in a month," he said. I nodded and hugged him one last time.

"I'll miss you," I said before we kissed for a long time.

"Come on, I have a party to go to," Dani complained.

"Bye," I said.

"Bye," he said kissing me quickly before getting on his bike and zooming off.

I went back up to my room, when I walked in and a guy was kneeling on the other bed in the room hanging a huge, beautiful photo of a waterfall on the wall.

"Um, hi," I said. He turned and we both laughed.

"Alex?"

"Carter?" he laughed, sitting on the bed. "What are you doing here?"

"This is my room," I said slowly, pointing at all my stuff.

"Uh, what?" We both pulled out our phones and checked our room assignments, then looked at one another's. Sure enough, we were roommates.

"I was wondering why my roommate had purple bedding, guess this makes more sense than a gay guy," he said standing. "So, I guess they made an admin error," he crossed his arms. His biceps bulged and I lost my train of thought for a second.

"Yeah," I said snapping out of it. "And this is a coed floor," I shrugged. "Should we talk to anyone or…" I trailed off.

"I'm cool with it if you are," he said slowly before taking his bedding out of a bag.

"All part of the experience, right?" I laughed taking my laptop out of its case.

"Exactly," he smiled, dressing his bed.

I took out the folder with pictures I was going to hang and took out the framed photo of Jag and I in Egypt on a camel.

"Is that your brother?" he asked, picking it up.

"Boyfriend," I said putting it back down on the dresser next to the head of my bed.

"Ah, yes, right, I remember, off limits, I respect it," he said folding clothes into his dresser. I smiled politely and nodded.

"So how long have you been dating?" he asked as we unpacked.

"About eleven months. He's coming up in a month for our one year, he's great," I said smiling.

"Oh, how long were you friends before that?" he said.

"We actually weren't. We met when I started a new school when I moved to Mass, and we actually met in an interesting way," I said, a slight laugh erupted after thinking about it.

"What?" he said laughing slightly.

"I have this really old pick-up truck and well, my door got stuck when I was getting out so I kicked it, and well it flew off and hit him riding his motor cycle," I said. He laughed and looked at me.

"Seriously?" he asked. I nodded and bit my lip. He laughed and sighed.

"That's funny," he smiled. I nodded and kneeled on my bed to hang photos. When I was done I sat on my bed and stretched.

"So how do you think this happened?" he asked.

"Well it is a coed dorm and I do have a male name," I shrugged and he nodded.

"Yo, Alex," two guys said coming in. Both were average height, one was on the skinnier side with red hair and green eyes, the other had a stockier build with shaggy, dirty blond hair and brown eyes.

"Oh, hello," the red head said looking at me.

"Dean, Heath, this is my roommate, Carter," Alex said looking at me.

"You're his roommate?" Dean, the red head, said looking at me.

"Yeah," I laughed shrugging.

"And I'm stuck with you," Heath, the dirty blond, said to Dean, a smirk on his face.

"So, what's up?" Alex smiled.

"Move in party in our room, you in or out?" he said to us.

"I'm in," I said getting up.

"Sick," Dean sang. I laughed and walked over.

"Come on," We all said. Alex shrugged and walked out. He locked the door behind us and we went into the next room where a bunch of people were already drinking and talking.

A few hours in my phone buzzed in my pocket and I looked at the screen, Jag. I smiled and went into the hall and pressed accept.

"Hey, babe," I said.

"Hey, I just dropped off Dani, wanted to see if your roommate came in yet," he said.

"Yeah," I said looking back at the party where Alex was talking with some guys from the floor.

"How is she?" he asked.

"She is kind of a he," I said slowly.

"What?" There was a banging sound in the background and I sighed.

"What did you break?" I asked.

"My chair," he sighed. I smiled and laughed a little. He sighed and started to laugh, too.

"Don't worry, I'm all yours," I said. He sighed and exhaled loudly.

"They made an admin error, but we don't care because it's all part of the experience, right?" I said. He sighed and I could picture him shrugging.

"Don't worry," I said.

"Okay," he sighed.

Chapter Sixteen

Alex

I saw Carter in the hall and I walked out. I was going to go ask her if she wanted a drink when I saw she was on the phone.

"I love you, okay?" she said. She laughed then smiled. "No, I can't wait to see you."

"Yeah, so when do you start at the bar?"

"Oh, cool tell Frank I say hi," she said.

"Don't go hitting on any hot girls that come in," she said. Then she laughed. "I love you more, okay?"

"K. Bye," she hung up and smiled at her phone.

I sighed and went back to the party. Carter came back in and walked over.

"I left my key inside, could I have yours?" she asked. I nodded and handed her my key.

"I'll be in soon, so leave it unlocked," I said. She nodded and walked out. A few minutes later I said bye and opened the door. Carter was pulling on a tank top over her black lace bra.

"Hey, thanks," she said, handing me my key before unhooking her bra under her shirt and pulling it out. Then she got into bed. I nodded and unbuttoned my shirt and tossed it on the ground and kicked off my jeans.

"Nice Batman boxers," she laughed.

"Hey, stop checking out my ass," I joked, getting into bed. She laughed and sighed. After some silence, I finally had to ask her what had been on my mind all night. "So, you really love your boyfriend, don't you?"

"Yeah," She replied, a smile on her face.

"When did you take those?" I asked trying to

change the subject, nodding towards the photos on the wall of them all over the world.

"He took me on a trip this past summer all over to the places I've always wanted to go."

"What a nice guy," I all but groaned.

"Yeah, he's the best," she smiled.

"Well, good night," I said.

"Night."

I woke up the next morning and rolled over, nearly falling off the bed. "Jesus Christ," I grumbled, propping myself up on my elbows.

"I did it too," Carter said softly. I looked over at her, she was sitting cross-legged on her bed, a cluster of pills in one hand and water bottle in the other.

"You're not a drug addict, are you?" I joked. She laughed, took the pills, took a swig of water then put the bottle down.

"They're for my anger issues," she said simply.

"Oh," I said slowly, nodding as I sat up and got out of bed.

"Nice morning wood," she laughed. I turned and bent over my bed, groaning into my pillow. Carter laughed again and I groaned louder.

"Great first morning, right?" I said into my pillow. She chuckled and patted me on the back. I turned my face to the side and she handed me a pair of sweatpants.

"I supposed I wouldn't have to worry about that with a girl roommate," she mused.

"Yeah," I laughed.

"I guess this will take some getting used to," she laughed before pulling a sweatshirt on over her tank top. "I'm going to go get food, want to come with?"

"Sure," I nodded, grabbing my key, ID, and a zip up hoodie. We walked down to the food court and filled our trays with almost the exact same breakfast and found a two-top table by a window.

"Want some coffee?" she asked, setting her tray down.

"Yes, thank you, I take it black," I said.

"Just like Jag," she smiled before heading over to the coffee station. I sighed and sat back, I needed to get over this girl. She came back over and put the mug down in front of me and took a sip of hers, holding it close to her lips. She inhaled and took another sip.

"Damn girl, just hook up an IV already," I joked.

"I would if I could," She said seriously, then she cracked a smile. We laughed and dug into our breakfasts.

After breakfast Carter went back to our room and I went over to Dean and Heath's. I walked in to Dean at his desk playing a video game on his laptop and Heath was lying on his bed, his laptop on his stomach.

"Hey man," Heath said, closing his laptop. Dean took his headphones off and turned in his chair.

"How's the insanely hot roommate," he said. Heath laughed and threw a foam football at Dean's head. Dean caught it before it hit him in the head and laughed at Heath.

"It's harder than you would think," I sighed, sitting on Heath's desk.

"And you're not just talking about your dick I'm guessing," Dean joked. I chuckled then sighed.

"This sucks, guys, I am so into her and she has a fucking boyfriend," I said, getting mad at myself for being in this situation.

"She has a boyfriend?" They both said in unison. They then looked at one another and laughed. I sighed and nodded.

"Their one year anniversary is in a month, he's coming up."

"Well let's fuck him up then!" Dean said. I laughed and shook my head.

"He sounds pretty badass," I admitted.

"Well we will just have to see about that," Dean smiled. Heath sighed and shook his head at his roommate.

The month flew by, soon enough it was Carter and Jag's anniversary, and he was coming up. I laid in bed for a while, facing the wall so Carter didn't know I was awake. She was up and cleaning the room, had been for an hour now. I thought about the past few weeks, they had been great. We all got along so well, Heath had started dating this girl Holly, Carter had made a friend—Jenny—in one of her classes and had brought her into the group. She was a tall blond with flawless skin, big blue eyes, and a perfect body. She didn't hold a candle to Carter's natural good looks, though. We were all sitting outside in the courtyard adjacent to our building trying to soak up the last of the Indian summer when the roar of a motorcycle engine came into earshot.

"Do you think that's him?!" Jenny said excitedly, sitting up from her spot on the blanket her and Carter were sharing. Carter sat up as well and looked at the hill. Sure enough a guy on a motorcycle came into view and she jumped up.

"That's him!" she squealed. Jenny clapped and jumped up as well, smoothing Carter's hair for her. Holly, who was sitting on Heath's lap in an Adirondack chair, looked at Carter and Jenny then at me, a sympathetic smile on her face. The motorcycle stopped in the lot by our dorm and the guy stood, took off his helmet and looked around. Carter waved then ran over and jumped into his arms, wrapping her legs around his waist. Dean patted me on the shoulder and Heath matched Holly's sympathetic smile.

"I'm so excited to meet him!" Jenny squealed, watching them and not us. Dean rolled his eyes and I smacked him on the chest with the back of my hand. Jenny was a sweet girl but slightly oblivious to the world around her. I looked over at Carter and Jag, they were currently making out, her fingers locked in his hair, his hands gripping her waist. I groaned and looked down.

"You can stay in our room tonight," Heath said softly. I nodded and thanked him. They walked over arm in arm, Carter was smiling up at him like a love-struck kid. He was tall, nowhere near as tall as me, but tall enough, with broad shoulders, tanned olive skin, a lean yet muscular build. He was handsome as hell, I couldn't deny it.

"Guys, this is my Jagger, Jag this is Jenny, Holly, Heath, Dean, and my roommate Alex," she smiled, her arms wrapped around his waist. He smiled and nodded at everyone then looked at Carter and she smiled. "We'll be upstairs, don't need us," she said before pulling him towards the dorm. Once they were inside I groaned and fell back in my chair.

A few hours later, I was walking back from class and I saw Jag leaning against the side of our dorm smoking a cigarette. His button down was partially unbuttoned over his bare chest and his hair was messier than before.

"Hey man, you're Car's roommate, right?" he asked, taking a drag. I nodded and shifted my backpack on my shoulder.

"Yeah."

"She's been good?" he smiled, eyes on me as smoke billowed out his nose. He looked so intimidating. Even though I was taller than him, he could easily take me.

"Like an angel," I said, smiling a tight smile before going inside. I went upstairs and opened the door. Carter was lying on the bed in her bra and underwear.

"Sorry, I'll be in the other room," I grumbled before walking out. I hated this, why did I have to be a wuss and not make a move? I went into the lounge and hung out till I saw them leave the room. I sighed and went into our room and got my books for my next class then headed downstairs. When I got outside they were sitting in one of the Adirondacks, Jag was smoking and Carter was in his lap, her arms around his shoulders.

"Hey, Alex," she smiled.

"Hey," I said.

"Want to have dinner with us tonight? We're going to the sushi bar down the road."

"Nah I'm good," I said.

"Please, come, I want you guys to get to know each other," she said taking my hand in hers.

"Fine," I sighed, smiling a tight smile.

"Good it's settled, meet us at 7," she smiled.

"Okay, bye," I called, already walking away from them.

At 7, I went down to the sushi bar and found Carter and Jag sitting at a table. I walked over and sat across from them. After two hours of the longest dinner of my life, we walked back to the dorm and went into the room.

"You don't have to sleep in Dean and Heath's room tonight, okay? I'm sorry we've been kind of kicking you out of your own room," she said when Jag was in the bathroom.

"No worries," I lied. She smiled and changed into her usual tank top and shorts and got into bed. Jag walked in, nodded at me, then pulled his shirt over his head, kicked off his jeans and got into bed with Carter. The lucky bastard, I hated him more than ever right now. I heard kissing noises and glanced over, she was on top of him and slowly kissing his neck and ear. I bit my lip and looked at the wall, turning on my side.

I woke up and Jag was sitting on the bed opening the window, Carter wasn't in the room.

"You don't mind if I smoke do you? It's cold out," he said.

"Not at all," I said getting up, pulling on a pair of jeans and a sweatshirt.

"You have class at 8?" he laughed.

"Yeah," I said grabbing my backpack.

"What school do you go to?" I asked, already knowing he didn't go to one.

"I don't go to school. I never really went in high school either. I'm working at a bar right now," he said taking a drag.

"Oh, short on cash?" I tried, trying to find something wrong with him.

"Nah, not at all, just bored," he shrugged. I sighed and nodded.

"Well I have class," I said, waving before taking off. I was walking out as Carter was walking in wearing a towel, holding her shampoo and conditioner.

"Hey," she smiled.

"Hi," I said.

"Is Jag up?" she asked. I nodded.

"Well, I have to go," I said. She nodded and then stopped me.

"This isn't weird, right?"

"Not at all, it's something we would eventually have to deal with," I shrugged. She nodded and sighed then smiled.

"Well, have fun at class," she said before going into our room.

I walked into class and sat down next to Heath in the lecture hall. "Hey man, how's it going?" he asked, taking out his notebook.

"My roommate, who I'm super into, is in love with a cool, 'dangerous' guy who rides a motorcycle, smokes, works at a bar just because he's bored, and could probably kick my ass if I tried anything," I sighed.

"That's rough, man," he mused, nodding slowly.

"I know," I sighed.

"What we need to do is find you a better girl," he said.

"Good luck with that," I laughed.

"What about Jenny?" he said, his eyes brightening. "Holly said she's into you," he urged, nudging me with his foot. I smiled and shrugged.

"She is gorgeous," I admitted. He laughed, slapping his hands together.

"See! There's a smile on your face already," he smiled.

Chapter Seventeen

Jagger

"Jag, can you go grab a fresh keg of Coors?" Frank asked, walking over. I nodded and went down to the basement and into the cooler. I grabbed a half keg and hoisted it onto my shoulder so it would be easier to walk upstairs. I went over to the keg room and tapped it, picking up the old one and bringing it out back. I went back into the bar and to the bathroom to wash my hands. I was walking back behind the bar when I did a double take. Frank was hugging Carter. Carter was here.

"Carter?!" I laughed, grabbing her up in a big hug. She squeezed me back then kissed me on the cheek.

"I handed in all my finals early and was able to come home sooner," she grinned, her hands gripping my shirt's sides.

"Oh, I am so happy to see you, this past month sucked without you," I said, kissing her forehead. She smiled and looked over at Frank.

"Can I steal my man?" she asked. He smiled and looked at us, nodding.

"Take all the time you can get with him," he said, winking at me. We both grinned and I grabbed my stuff and we left. As soon as we were outside I pulled her into my arms, kissing her passionately. She gripped my sides as I deepened the kiss, caressing her cheek with one hand, the other gripping her lower back. When I finally pulled back she was nearly out of breath. I smiled and kissed her again, this time a quick peck, and wrapped my arm around her shoulder.

"I am so glad you are back," I sighed, opening her truck door for her.

"Me too," she grinned before getting in.

We went to my parents' house, where I was still staying, and walked inside. The house was overrun with Christmas decorations, making everything smell like pine needles and cinnamon.

"Wow," Carter laughed, looking up at the huge tree tucked into the curve of the stairs, decorated in silver and gold ornaments.

"Just wait, there are like, eleven trees throughout the house," I whispered in her ear. She laughed and shook her head in disbelief.

"Trina doesn't half-ass anything, that's for sure," she said, and I laughed and threw my arm around her.

"You hungry?" I asked, and she shot me a look.

"When am I not?" she asked, and we laughed as we walked arm in arm into the huge kitchen. "Jesus, I missed this pantry," she said, going into the walk-in pantry that was stocked with everything you could ever want. I smiled and watched her pull down two packs of microwave popcorn, a bag of M&M's, and a bottle of soda.

"Movie night?" I asked and she smiled and nodded. We made the popcorn and I carried all the snacks down to the theater. It was one of my favorite parts of the estate—a small movie theater in the basement. It had three rows of large, black leather recliners in pairs of two, a small aisle between the sets of seats. We sat in the middle row and she threw her legs over my lap, tossing some popcorn into her mouth. I picked up the tablet that controlled the screen and we picked a movie.

After the movie was over we went upstairs where we ran into my mom in the kitchen. She smiled when she saw Carter.

"Carter, dear, how are you?" she asked, grinning wildly as she hugged Carter.

"Good, thanks, Mrs. Hastings," she smiled.

"How was your first semester of college?"

"Amazing, thank you," she smiled, squeezing my hand.

"How long are you in town for? Please tell me you are bringing her to the holiday events," she said, looking at me now.

"I don't even want to go to those," I laughed, running my fingers through my hair. Carter smacked my arm with the back of her hand and smiled at my mom.

"Of course I'll be there, Mrs. Hastings," she smiled. My mom's whole face lit up and she grasped Carter's hands.

"Oh, I am so happy, and please, dear, call me Trina," she smiled before squeezing Carter's hands, then she patted my shoulder and went off into her office.

Once we were in my bedroom, Carter turned to look at me. "What did I just get myself into?" she laughed, wrapping her arms around my neck.

"Oh, my dear girlfriend, you just got yourself into the worst string of holiday parties and formal dinners that you will ever experience in your entire life," I said before kissing the tip of her nose. She groaned and then we both laughed and she wrapped her legs around me, effectively koala-bearing herself onto me. I smiled and walked into the closet, holding her against me as I grabbed a t-shirt and pair of boxer shorts for her to wear to bed and kicked off my shoes, still holding her. She nuzzled her nose into my neck and collar bone and I smiled and held her as I walked from the closet to the bathroom. I placed her down on the counter and began to wash up for bed. She hopped down and opened the medicine cabinet on the left side of the sink where her toiletries she had left were. She smiled and began to brush her teeth. I looked over at her, my mouth covered in toothpaste foam and she looked at me, same foamy lips. I laughed and she smiled, rinsing her mouth.

We finished getting ready for bed and once she was dressed in my t-shirt and rolled up boxers, we got into my bed.

"So, really, what did I get myself into?" she asked, looking over at me. I rolled onto my side to face her and propped myself up on my elbow.

"Well, there's the Christmas Eve soiree, then the Christmas Day dinner party, and finally the New Year's Eve gala," I said. She laughed and then groaned, raking her fingers through her hair. "Get ready to eat a lot of overly fancy food and talk to some really boring people."

"Well at least there's food," she shrugged, then laughed.

On Christmas Eve, I was in my closet getting ready when Carter walked in. She was wearing a red sweater dress with a turtleneck and long sleeves, black tights, and high heeled green ankle boots.

"Well don't you look festive?" I said, giving her a quick kiss. She smiled and sat on one of the benches.

"I was about to say the same to you," she joked, I was currently fresh out of the shower, only a towel wrapped around my waist.

"I thought this would be a good look," I shot back and she smiled, crossing her legs and leaning back. I pulled down a hunter green, cable knit, cowl neck sweater and a pair of clean jeans and got dressed.

"You clean up nice, Hastings," she said, standing and walking over to me. I smiled and wrapped my arms around her, pulling her into a deep kiss.

"Gross," Juliet joked, walking into my closet. She was wearing an olive-green blouse and black skirt, a color that complimented her slightly olive toned skin. We both got our complexions from our father, mom had the skin color of a porcelain doll.

"Hey, Jules," Carter smiled, then she looked back at me and blushed, swiping her thumb over my bottom lip. I saw a swatch of lipstick on her thumb and she rubbed her fingers together, smiling at me.

"Ready for bore-fest?" Juliet joked, and Carter smiled.

"Let's get this over with," I said, wrapping my arm around Carter's waist, following Juliet out of my closet.

By New Year's Eve, Carter had already met the regulars that attended these annual events—mostly business associates of my parents or long-established family friends. Tonight was the gala, an event hosted at one of my father's client's hotels located in Boston. It was an event my mom helped host every year. Carter arrived at my house around 4 and she, Juliet, Juliet's friend Caroline, and I all took one of the limos mom had commissioned for the event up to Boston. We got to the hotel and I checked us all into our rooms then we went upstairs. At 7 we were waiting by the elevator bank for Juliet and Caroline. I looked at Carter, who was absolutely stunning in a strapless, muted gold floor length dress, her hair up in an elegant twist. She was fixing the lapels of my fitted suit jacket when Juliet and Caroline waltzed down the hall, arm in arm. Once we were all together we headed down to the event hall.

At five minutes to midnight Carter found me sitting at the bar. I had been watching her all night, dancing and joking with Juliet and her friend. I wasn't big on dancing, and she knew that, so we had an understanding at situations like this. She stood between my legs, wrapping her arms around my neck. Just then a slow song came on and she looked at me, a small smile on her face.

"Dance with me?" she asked softly. I smiled and sighed, knowing I couldn't say no to her, and finished my drink then let her lead me onto the dance floor. She positioned my hands on her waist, placing hers around my neck, and we began to sway and step to the slow, melodic beat.

"Thank you for going to all these stupid events," I said, my chin resting on her head, which was tucked towards my shoulder.

"Of course," she replied, giving my neck a quick kiss. I smiled and kissed the top of her head. "This is going to be our year, I just know it," she mused. I pulled her closer and held her a bit tighter. I loved this girl uncontrollably. The countdown began and we parted to look at the wall where there was a projected live stream of the NYC ball drop. At midnight, balloons dropped from the ceiling and Carter looked up at me.

"Happy New Year," she smiled before kissing me.

Chapter Eighteen

Carter

It had been two months since I had seen Jag. School had picked up since returning from winter break. I finally had a free weekend and was caught up on homework, so I decided to drive up to visit him. He was working late that night so I went to the bar to surprise him at work, feeling more excited than ever to see him. I walked in and my heart broke. I saw Jag, leaning over a bar with a blond girl on the other side of the bar, making out with him. Her hands were clutching his face, and she was wearing a skimpy black dress, nearly exposing her ass as she leaned further over the tall bar.

"Jason Fucking Hastings," I yelled. He pulled back and his jaw dropped. Every single person in the bar was silent.

"Carter," he said, running out from behind the bar, his face pale, a smear of cheap, pink lipstick across his lips.

"Asshole!" I slapped him, hard. He staggered back and looked at me, those big green eyes of his were wide—with anger or shock I couldn't tell. The bar patrons "ooh'ed" and "aah'ed" and the girl looked mortified.

"Well, I see how it is," I spat as the blond girl ran over to him. "We're over."

"Carter, wait," he called as I ran out.

"No, you cheated on me and I can never forgive you for that!" I shouted, getting in my truck. My blood was on fire, and my lungs stung with every sharp breath I inhaled. I knew if I looked at him any longer I would lose it.

"Carter, it's not what it looks like," he called, running up to my truck. "I promise you, just let me explain," he pleaded as he caught up to me.

"Don't bother, it's always exactly what it looks like," I spat.

"No, it's not," He was holding on to my door.

"Were you not kissing her?" I asked simply. How I was composing myself I had no idea.

"No but—," he started, his cheeks were turning a harsh, unforgiving red.

"And is that not cheating on me?" I asked, trying to keep that composure. My blood was coursing through my veins hot and fast, my fists tightened around the steering wheel. I tried to do my deep breathing exercises.

"No but—."

"No buts, it's over," I hit reverse, his hands fell back from the door, and I peeled out.

I waited till I got home to cry. I drove all the way back to New York, dry eyed and fists tight on the wheel. I ran up to my room and slammed the door behind me, tears streaming down my face. Dean, Alex, and Jenny were sitting on the floor doing work.

"Carter, what's wrong?" Jenny said, jumping up. I crawled into bed and she climbed in after me, hugging me.

"Guys, give us a minute," she said. They nodded and patted my back before walking out. "What happened? I thought you were going to visit Jag?" she whispered softly, tucking my hair away from my face.

"I did," I sobbed.

"And?" she wiped my tears gently with the pads of her thumbs.

"And I caught him kissing a blonde skank," I cried, my chest racking with sobs and shaky breaths.

"Are you sure I can't do anything?" Alex walked in.

"Out," Jenny yelled at him. He backed out, hands in front of his chest and closed the door.

"I'm so sorry, hon. You're too good for him," she cooed, returning to her nurturing mode before she hugged me. I started to cry harder and she held me tighter. A few minutes later, Alex poked his head in.

"Jen, Rick is here for your date," he said quietly.

"Shit, I forgot about that. I can stay," she said, the last part softer and directed towards me. I shook my head and she sighed and nodded.

"Take over," she said to Alex. He nodded and walked over slowly.

"Bye, sweetheart," she said, squeezing my arm. Alex sat down where Jenny was and I rested my head on his shoulder, my arms around his neck.

"I heard through the door, I'm so sorry," he said into my hair. I started to cry even harder and he held me tighter. Whether it was from the pure exhaustion after driving nearly seven hours straight, or the lack of oxygen from all the crying, I drifted off before I even knew what was happening.

I woke up and sat up. Alex was lying in my bed, asleep, a big salt-water stain from my tears on his shirt. I got up and saw the picture of Jag and me in Greece and a rush of anger flowed through me. I grabbed it and smashed it on the ground. Alex shot up and looked at me then the ground.

"Did you take your meds?" he asked softly.

"No, I ran out. I have a med check with my new doctor this week," I said grabbing my trash bin and dust pan. I cleaned up the mess and Alex helped me take down all the pictures of Jag and me on my wall.

"Come on, let's do something fun today," Alex said changing his shirt. I smiled and hugged him.

"Thank you for being there," I said.

"I'll always be here," he said. I smiled and let go and grabbed my stuff.

"Let's go," I said.

He rounded up the guys, all half asleep, and I texted Jenny. We all met down in the quad and took the train into the city. I was sitting in between Jenny and Alex, across from us was Heath and Holly, and in the row next to us was Pat, Dean, and Jeremy—one of Pat's friends. We all walked out into Grand Central and made our way into the busy city streets. We all had been talking about making a trip into the city, we went to school a mere 20 minutes away, and had yet to do a trip. Jenny and I intertwined our hands and swung them back and forth as we made our way to Times Square. Heath and Holly were up ahead, his arm around her thin shoulders. Alex walked with Pat, heads bent towards each other, talking in hushed tones. Dean and Jeremy were behind us, talking loudly about a professor they had together. We made it to Times Square and I smiled and looked around, I had never been.

"So, you're telling me you have been to all those places, but never New York City?" Jeremy laughed in disbelief. I nodded, laughing. We were all sitting at a cluster of tables outside a café, the huge screens of Times Square flashing all around us.

"Yes, I moved to Massachusetts from Oregon, I didn't grow up around here," I shrugged.

"You're from Oregon?!" Heath, Jeremy, and Pat all said loudly. I laughed.

"Yes, you guys. What is the big deal about Oregon?" I said. They shrugged, looking at one another.

"Just a weird state," Heath said. Holly giggled and tucked a piece of his shaggy hair behind his ear.

"It is not a weird state!" I laughed. He shrugged and looked at me.

"Oregon is definitely a weird state," Jeremy agreed.

"Have any of you ever even been there?" I asked. They all looked at one another. No one spoke. "Exactly, so don't knock my hometown, dicks," I said. They all laughed and I smiled.

We finished our meal and walked out. I hung back and waited for Alex to walk out the door.

"Thank you, for this, for everything," I smiled, bumping my elbow into his side playfully. He smiled and nodded.

"What are friends for?" he said, wrapping his arm around my shoulders and squeezing. Jenny looked back at us and smiled a big smile. I smiled back, looking at all my people. I never had this, not back in Oregon, not in high school, not even with my own family. Jag had been it, and now he was gone, and I had these amazing people here. These were my true friends, my family.

Chapter Nineteen

Carter

A few weeks later Alex and I were sitting on the floor of our room eating sushi when there was a knock on the door.

"I'll get it," I said, getting up and smoothing out my skirt as I walked over to the door. I opened it and Jag was standing there in an army uniform.

"What the fuck?" I blurted. Alex stood and walked up behind me.

"I tried calling you," he said taking off his cap to reveal a buzz cut. I suddenly had the urge to run my fingers through his now-absent shaggy black curls. This feeling left me uncomfortable.

"Yeah, I know," I crossed my arms.

"There was no other way but to come up and tell you in person that I joined the army. I'm shipping out to finish my training tomorrow," he said. I felt the sushi churn in my stomach.

"Alex, give us a minute?" I whispered, my eyes trained on Jag.

"You'll be okay?" he asked. I nodded and he stepped out. Jag walked in and I closed the door. I leaned against my desk and looked him up and down. He seemed bigger, more muscular—even his posture had straightened, making him seem taller. He looked around the room, most likely noticing the absence of all the photos with him in them. He rung his cap in his hands and looked at me.

"Why did you join the army?" I sighed, breaking the silence.

"Because I had no other reason to stay here but you. You gave my life meaning, and when you left

me... I have no purpose. No reason to be here."
His words felt like a punch to the gut.

"Jesus, Jason," I groaned, sitting on my desk chair. He sighed and scratched his now buzzed head.

"I still love you, Carter," he admitted quietly.

"Well I don't love you anymore. I haven't since I saw you kissing the girl in the bar," I said running my fingers through my hair. He looked distraught. "I can't let myself go back there." I said softly, knowing that what I said before wasn't true, seriously hoping he couldn't tell, though. No matter how much I tried, I still loved him. He was my first and only love. I would always love him, but not the way I used to after what had happened.

"Just so you know, that girl at the bar, she was at her bachelorette party. Her friends made this bucket list for her, one item was to kiss a bartender. Her friend is a regular at Franks, she explained all of it after you left. She kissed me for a second, you walked in, and the rest is history," he sighed. My heart broke all over again.

I looked up at him. I could feel the sadness in him, just by looking at his eyes. He looked at the sushi dinner for two on the floor and scoffed under his breath.

"So, you're with Alex now," he said nodding towards the sushi dinner.

"No! We were just having dinner together, he's my friend," I said crossing my arms.

"He's in love with you. Are you that oblivious?" he spat. I slapped him. Where did he think he had the right to talk to me like that? He gripped his reddening cheek, his eyes wide. I was getting déjà vu from the night we broke up, it was all making me sick to my stomach.

"Get out of my room, get out of my dorm, get out of this city, just get out," I yelled. Hot tears sprung up in the corners of my eyes.

"I'm sorry." he rubbed his cheek and replaced his cap. He was about to leave when I sighed and grabbed his arm.

"Just, please be careful," I whispered.

He nodded and looked me over one last time, kissed my cheek softly, then left. I fell to the ground and wrapped my arms around my knees. Alex walked in and sat next to me, wrapping his arms around me. I leaned my head on his shoulder and leaned into the comforting hug. It was just what I needed.

After a while I composed myself, cleaned my face, and looked at him, "He said something," I said sitting up.

"Yeah?"

"He said that you liked me," I said slowly.

"Yeah, and?"

"Well… Do you?" I looked at the ground.

"I mean, kinda. I did when we first met," he said slowly, his eyes fixed on the ground. He didn't say if he still felt that way, though. We sat in silence for a few minutes before I sighed.

"I'm sorry, Alex. I didn't know," I said slowly. "I thought we were friends. From day one, when we met at accepted student's day, I always just thought we were friends," I said, looking down then at him.

"I'm sorry too, and we are friends," he said, smiling a tight smile. "I'll be okay, and you'll be okay, and we're friends," he nodded. I nodded and we cleaned up our dinner and sat at our desks, pretending to do work and ignoring the tension vibrating between our turned backs.

I laid in bed that night and waited for Alex to fall asleep. Once he had been snoring for a while, I got out of bed quietly and crouched beside it, pulling out a small shoe box. I sat at my desk, the cold wood of the chair on my bare skin sent goose bumps running over my entire body. I opened the box and sighed—I hadn't looked in this box in weeks. I took out the photos, the ticket stubs from our trips, and at the bottom of the box was the tape he had given me. It was the first thing he had ever given me. I looked at the trash can next to my desk and contemplated throwing it all out. But something deep down was telling me not to.

I sat there for a while, looking through the photos, reminiscing about the memories. Then I stopped. It was a photo of us at Frank's bar one day, it was him, Frank, and me all behind the bar, smiling. He had taught me how to make an old fashioned that day. But the next memory stung, and left a bitter taste in my mouth. It was him, kissing the girl, leaning over that exact same bar we were all grinning behind. I put the photos in the back of the box and tucked it back under the bed.

I climbed back into bed and fell asleep doing everything I could in my power to not think of Jag. I woke up to voices. Blinking at the light, I propped myself up on my elbows and looked around. Pat, Heath, and Jenny were at the door, Alex blocking it.

"She's sleeping," Alex said.

"Just wake her up, we're getting breakfast! Pancakes, Alex, they solve everything!" Jenny said, clapping her hands. That girl did love pancakes. I laughed and they all looked back at me.

"I'm up now," I smiled, sitting up.

"See, perfect, now we can go," Jenny smiled, walking past Alex. He gave me an "I tried," look and I shrugged my shoulders.

Jenny handed me a pair of leggings and I pulled them on then climbed out of bed. I grabbed a sweatshirt and pulled it on over my tank top and slipped on a pair of moccasins. We all piled in to Alex's Jeep, him and Pat up front, Jenny, Heath, and me in the back. He drove to the small breakfast place we all frequented and we walked in. We took the big booth in the back and looked at the large plastic menus.

"What should I get?" Jenny said, looking at the menu. We all exchanged looks.

"Pancakes," we all said in unison. We laughed and she smacked Alex with the menu. He held his hands up and she laughed. I smiled and looked around the table at my friends. Pat elbowed Heath and he spilled orange juice on himself. Jenny was contemplating the number of pancakes she should get, and Alex was guzzling coffee. I smiled, I was happy—truly, honest to God happy.

"Thanks guys," I smiled.

"For what?" Pat said, looking up from his coffee. He was Alex's best friend from home, and mostly hung out with people from his classes. But occasionally, he would come along with us. Alex gave him a look and Pat gave him one back. Heath smiled and nodded at me, and Jenny squeezed my hand.

"We love you, Carter. You're one of us, and we're family," Jenny smiled. I put my arm around her and squeezed.

"I've never really had a group of friends before, so it's weird for me, but I love you guys," I smiled. The boys all fake awed and then nodded at me, smiling. I smiled and we all went back to our breakfast.

Chapter Twenty

Carter

It was freezing out and there was a storm brewing. It made me think of the storm when Jag and I stayed at the trailer. I sighed, my steps slowing down as I thought of him. It had been two months since he came and told me he was enlisted and leaving. I stopped walking, I needed to stop thinking about him. It started to drizzle and I started to jog, trying to get inside before the storm hit. I didn't make it, not even close. I was three dorms away when it started to pour rain, I was soaking wet by the time I got to only two dorms away. A car pulled up next to me and I saw it was Pat.

"Need a ride?" he called out to me. I nodded, and all but jumped into his Suburban.

"Here," he handed me a sweatshirt from the backseat.

"Thanks," I shivered, pulling it on. It was like a dress on me.

"So, why don't you drive to classes? I mean, we live in New England," he chuckled.

"I thought I could make it back in time, and I like my parking spot," I laughed. He laughed and smiled, glancing over at me then looking at the road. I looked at him and the top of his head grazed the roof of the car. Like Alex, he was freakishly tall.

"So, why do you think that you, Alex, and all your friends are so tall? Is it like something in the water you drink?" I joked.

"Maybe, I don't know. I think it's the basketball camp we went to, they put us on one of those medieval stretchers," he joked. I laughed and he smiled and laughed, too. We pulled up in front of my building and he looked at me.

"Want to go out to dinner, maybe get some coffee?" he asked.

"Sure, let me just go change into dry clothes," I smiled, nodding.

"Cool, I'll be here," he said.

I smiled and nodded. I ran inside and unlocked my door. Alex was taking a nap. I undressed and quickly and carefully, as to not wake him up, changed into my nice black lace bra and underwear then pulled on a pair of nice skinny jeans. I grabbed a sweater then pulled on my leather jacket and sat on my bed to slip on my lace up boots. When I grabbed my purse off my desk the strap snagged the stapler and it clattered to the floor. Alex woke up and looked at the floor where the stapler had fallen then at me.

"Where are you off to?" he said, rubbing his eyes.

"Dinner."

"Oh, with who?" he sat up.

"Pat," I checked my hair and make-up.

"Like a date?"

"I don't know," I shrugged. "Well, bye," I smiled as I walked out. I pulled on my hood and ran out back to his car. He smiled and we left. He took me to a quiet, intimate restaurant called Car-michaels right outside the city and we got a corner booth.

"How did you find this place?" I asked, looking around at the rustic décor.

"I know the owners?" he grinned, waggling his eyebrows at me.

"How so?" I asked.

"They're my brothers." He smiled a wide smile.

"Really?" I laughed. He smiled and nodded. "That's so cool," I smiled. A tall guy that looked like Pat walked over.

"Hey, Mike, this is Carter. Carter, this is my older brother, Mike," he said.

"It's nice to meet you," he smiled shaking my hand.

"You, too," I smiled, "You've got a lovely place here."

"Why, thank you. And it seems my brother has an even lovelier date." I blushed and he smiled and wished us a good meal, then excused himself.

We finished eating, he paid, then we ran back through the rain to his car hand in hand. Overall it was a great night. He parked outside my dorm and looked at me.

"Thanks for dinner," I smiled.

"It was fun," he said.

"Maybe we could do it again some time, like Friday night?" he said, leaning in slightly.

"I'd like that," I leaned in more.

"I'll pick you up at 8," he said, I could feel his breath on my cheek.

"Okay," I breathed before kissing him. He kissed me back softly, his thumb and forefinger holding my chin. We parted briefly and I smiled, biting my lip before kissing him again. When we parted again he smiled, his eye lids at half-mast.

"I'll see you on Friday," he murmured, his cheeks hot.

"Friday," I smiled before getting out and running in.

"How was it?" Alex asked, walking in as I was getting into bed.

"It was good, were going out again on Friday," I said pulling on my sweatshirt.

"Cool," he nodded, getting into bed.

"Yeah," I smiled.

"So how did this happen?"

"I was running back from class in the middle of the storm, and he was driving by and picked me up," I explained. He nodded and laid back. I ignored the tension once again.

Pat and I had been dating for a month now, after the first two dates we barely left each other's sides.

We had yet to be intimate, the burn of Jag's infidelity still left a bad taste in my mouth. However, tonight was the night. I got back from class around 6 and we were going out at 7:30. I showered and let my hair dry curly as I changed into my cute lace underwear. I was sitting on my bed in my bra and panties moisturizing my legs when Alex walked in.

"Oh, sorry," he said, about to step out.

"No come in, sorry," I smiled sheepishly, pulling one of Pat's t-shirts I had taken over my head. He nodded slowly and walked in.

"One month anniversary, huh?" he said. I smiled and nodded. I got up and sat at my desk to do my make-up then undid my hair from the knot I had it in and shook it out. I stood and pulled on a black, long sleeve top and a pair of tight blue jeans. I slipped on my leather jacket then stepped into my ankle boots.

"You look, wow," Alex said running his fingers through his hair. I smiled and blushed.

"Thanks," I laughed. There was a knock on the door and I bit my lip and opened the door. Pat was standing there in a button down, a pair of nice jeans, and a sports coat.

"Wow, Carter, you look, wow," he said. I laughed and looked at Alex, who had nearly said the same thing.

"What?" Pat smiled, looking at us.

"Sometimes I forget that you guys have known each other your entire lives," I smiled, kissing Pat on the cheek.

"Oh, did we have a moment?" Pat said, looking at Alex. Alex laughed and nodded.

"What?" I laughed, looking from one to another.

"We would always say the same stuff or do the same thing, and our parents called it us having a 'moment'," Pat smiled, his arm around me. Alex nodded, laughing.

"Teachers hated us all 12 years of school," he laughed, his hands shoved in his front pockets.

"That they did. Ready, Car?" Pat said, looking down at me.

I smiled and nodded. We said bye to Alex and left.

He took me to a nice restaurant in the middle of the city then we walked around a bit. He bought a pint of our favorite ice cream, and we went back to his dorm and up to his single room. We watched a movie and ate ice cream. It was a perfect, simple night. Then finally, as the film ended, he leaned over and kissed me, slowly easing my jacket off my shoulders. I unbuttoned his shirt with shaky, yet confident fingers, and tossed it on the floor. We laughed and kissed and caressed each other, safe in the cocoon of his small bedroom. I woke up at 9 A.M. and looked at him asleep next to me. I carefully got out of bed and got dressed. I leaned over and kissed his forehead. He blinked and looked at me.

"I have class," I smiled, sitting on his bed.

"Oh," he said, sitting up.

"Yeah, but I had a lot of fun last night."

"Yeah, me too," he smiled. I leaned down and kissed him on the lips.

"See you later," I said. He nodded and smiled. I waved and walked out.

Chapter Twenty-One

Pat

A few days after mine and Carter's anniversary, Alex and I were walking back to his dorm from class when I finally brought up Carter.

"You're my best friend, man, and I hate not being able to talk to you about my girlfriend," I sighed, nudging him with my elbow.

"You can," he said looking at me. I gave him a look and he shot me one right back. Half of our conversations went like this, half spoken, half unspoken, communicated through our knowing looks.

"But I thought you, 'ya know, liked her and stuff," I said shifting my bag on my shoulder.

"I did, but I never had a shot with her. I was in the friend zone from day one," he said. I sighed and shrugged.

"She really cares about you," I said. He smiled slightly and let out a strained chuckle.

"Yeah, if only in a different way, but I'm over it, so we can talk," he said. I looked at him, and I just knew. I knew he was putting his feelings aside for me.

"You sure?" I asked. He nodded and shoved me.

"Best friends since kindergarten and we never let a girl get between us. Let's not start now," he said. I smiled and nodded.

"You're right, you're absolutely right," I agreed.

"So how was your anniversary?" he asked.

"Amazing," I smiled.

"Good," he laughed. "She came back the next day so I guess it was better than good," he joked. I smiled and shrugged.

"I really like this girl, man. Like, I think I'm in love with her," I said smiling. He smiled and nodded.

"Trust me, I know how easy it is to fall for her. I don't blame you," I said. He laughed and patted me on the back. He opened the dorm door and Jenny and Carter were sitting on Carter's bed doing homework.

"Hey," Carter smiled, going on her knees on her already elevated bed to kiss me.

"Hey," I smiled. Alex put his bag on the floor by his bed and I dropped mine by their dressers.

"How was class?" Jenny said putting her book on Carter's desk, which was at the end of her bed.

"Long, our professor is like 200 years old," Alex said, taking out his camera and laptop. Jenny giggled a little more than was necessary and smiled. He smiled and sat at his desk, plugging in his computer to upload his photos from his portfolio class.

"Hey, Alex, can I borrow you for some shots with Jenny?" Carter said.

"Sure," Alex said, his eyes on his computer screen, not even turning around to look at her.

"Thanks," Carter smiled.

"Hey, why not me?" I laughed.

"It's an intimate shot. I don't think that you would be okay with kissing Jenny," she laughed. "You cool with that, Alex?" she said leaning to see past me. He still didn't move. I smiled, knowing how he got with his art.

"Yeah," he waved it off, his eyes on his screen.

"He gets so intense with his photography," Jenny laughed, putting her stuff in her bag.

"He always has," I said. She smiled and shouldered her bag.

"See you tomorrow morning for the shoot," she said, saying bye to Carter.

"Yeah, 8 A.M., I'll have outfits for you already so just wear a strapless bra and nude underwear," she said. Jenny nodded and waved bye.

"What's Jenny's here for?" I asked, sitting next to Carter on her bed.

"Painting and figure drawing, but she wants to be a model," she said. I nodded and laid down, and she put my head in her lap and smiled at me. I smiled and she ran her fingers through my hair. "Alex, want to order in Chinese?"

"Yeah sure," he said, face trained on his laptop screen.

"Wow he's really fixated on his work," Carter laughed, grabbing her phone.

She dialed our regular Chinese food place and ordered all our usual items. We watched TV until food came then peeled Alex away from the computer long enough to eat.

"I should get back to my room," I said. She nodded and walked me outside.

"See you tomorrow," she said.

"I don't have any classes till 11. Could I come to the shoot with you?" I asked.

"Sure," she smiled.

"Should I meet you here?" I asked. She nodded, kissed me, we said our byes and parted.

The next day I met up with Carter, Alex, and Jenny. Carter was wearing overall shorts over see through black tights, Converses, and a black long sleeve shirt. Her hair was pinned up on her head, a few curly strands framing her face, her camera was hanging around her neck.

"You look pretty," I said kissing her. She smiled and twirled her keys on her hand and picked up a duffle.

"Ready?" she said. I took the bag from her and she smiled and wrapped her arm around my waist. We got in her truck and she drove to an old, broken down brick factory building with broken windows and graffiti.

"This place is sick," I said as Alex and I carried her stuff into the factory.

"Okay, Alex, change into this button down. Jenny, this outfit," she said handing them both clothing. They changed then waited for further instructions.

"Here," Carter said handing her a lipstick. Jenny put it on then Carter pocketed it. She took the first few pictures of Jenny in a broken window-sill, the light streaming in made Jenny look cool, and the shots were amazing. Then she brought in Alex and posed them. Finally, a few hours later they were done and we loaded everything into her truck and got a late breakfast before going back to campus. Carter dropped off Alex and Jenny at the dorm and drove me to class.

"I think Jenny likes Alex," she said as she walked me inside.

"I know she does," I smiled and kissed her. "Should we set them up?"

"Why not?," she laughed. She smiled and pulled me close.

"See you later," I said. She nodded and kissed me one last time before going back to her truck. I smiled, shaking my head slowly, thinking *how did I get so lucky to get a girl like her?* as I walked into my class.

Chapter Twenty-Two

Carter

*P*at, Alex, and Jenny helped me load my stuff into my truck a few hours before I had to leave for home. The past four months had sped by, and it was the end of the school year. I was the last one to finish packing, so we all went out for lunch together before Dean and Jenny carpooled back to Connecticut and Heath and Holly went to Holly's house in Long Island. Alex and Pat were caravanning back to Vermont, they were the last to leave with me.

"I love you," Pat said, kissing me again.

He was leaning in my truck window for our 10-minute long good-bye.

"I love you too, now go before Alex flips," I laughed. He smiled and kissed me one last time before getting into his Suburban. Alex closed the trunk and walked over.

"So, you're rooming with Jenny next year," he said. I sighed and nodded.

"And you're rooming with Pat, so it's all good," I smiled. He shrugged and nodded.

"I'll miss ya, roomie," I said.

"You, too," he smiled.

"Till next year," I smiled, hugging him.

"Till next year," he repeated. We hugged then he smiled and got in his car and they left. I pulled out after them and started on my three hour drive home.

When I got home I heard loud music from the back yard and went around back. Dani was in the pool with a bunch of her friends.

"Sis!" she laughed drunkenly, running over to hug me.

"Don't hug me, you're wet," I said, my hands up. She giggled and jumped back into the pool.

"How's the super-hot boyfriend?" she asked, once she resurfaced from below the water.

"He's good," I smiled. She laughed and started playing with her friends again so I started to unload my truck.

I hadn't been back in my room since Jag and I broke up. There were pictures everywhere, his stuff all over the place, and stuff he gave me. I threw out all the pictures and put all his stuff in a box and went down stairs. I drove over to his parent's house, walked over to the door and knocked. It opened and Juliet stood there wearing all black, her eyes puffy.

"Carter, what are you doing here? Did you hear?" she said, a tear rolling down her cheek.

"No, hear what?" I asked, confused, shifting the box from one hip to the other.

"They lost communication with Jason's platoon a few weeks ago, and they can only assume that he's… dead. A couple officers came to talk to us today," she sobbed. I dropped the box on the marble step and looked at her.

"You're not kidding. Oh my God," I breathed. I felt empty, yet as if I were bursting at the seams all at once.

"No," she cried. We hugged for a long time, both of us taking turns crying and consoling one another

"So, what did you come by for?" she asked after we collected ourselves.

"I just got back from school and I wanted to bring over all of his stuff he left," I said slowly. She nodded and took the box, hugging it to her chest.

"I'm so sorry, Juliet," I said. She nodded and we exchanged our byes and I left.

I went back to my truck and got in slowly. I sat in the driveway for a long time, my mind blank. Jag was dead. He was gone. I hadn't thought about him in a long time, and I felt a sudden rush of guilt. It was all my fault. He joined the army because of me. He left and went to war because of me. He was dead. I would never see him again.

I pulled it together, drove home, and went up to my bedroom. I ran to the trash can and pulled out all the photos, as if I was expecting them to not even be there. I dug through all my stuff, which was piled in the middle of my floor, and found the shoe box. I put the box on my bed and put the photos in it. I put the box in my closet and sighed, hugging myself. Then I remembered something.

I went over to my desk and opened the bottom drawer, moving the papers and pens out of the way to pull the photograph I knew was at the bottom out. It was from the first time he was in my bedroom, out first photo together. I sunk to the floor, hugging my knees to my chest. I looked at the photo for a long time. We were so happy and in love. I wiped my eyes and sighed.

"Good-bye, Jason," I whispered, before placing the photo back into its safe hiding place and stood, closing the drawer. He was gone and it was time to officially move on, this time for good.

Epilogue

Carter: Three Years Later

"I love this place," I said looking around our new apartment. Pat, Jenny, Alex, and I had all graduated this May and found a large two-bedroom apartment in the city.

"Me, too," Pat smiled putting a box of my clothes on the counter.

"And I love you," I hugged him. He smiled and kissed my forehead.

"Get a room," Jenny laughed, carrying in boxes.

"They did," Alex joked, coming up behind her and kissing her cheek. She blushed and smiled. In the middle of sophomore year, Alex and Jenny got together and have been together since. After school, Jenny got modeling jobs and Alex worked at the same agency as her as a photography intern. Pat got a job at a comic book company as one of the artists, and I was working as a freelance photographer with some agencies.

"This place is amazing," Jenny smiled, coming in from the large balcony. "Carter, you could get some amazing shoots done out here," she said, hugging me. I smiled and hugged her back.

"I know, when the Realtor showed Pat and me the place, that's the first thing I thought," I said, putting some dishes away.

"I feel really good about this," Jenny smiled.

"Me too," I nodded.

A few weeks later I had some models over for a photo shoot when there was a knock on the door.

"Is anyone missing?" I said, confused. The models all looked at one another and shrugged, shaking their heads. "Hang on then, I'll be right back," I said, walking off the terrace where the shoot was set up and over to the front door. I opened it and felt my heart stop, stomach drop, and lungs dry up. I couldn't move. I couldn't breathe. I was hallucinating, I was sure of it.

"Jag?" I gasped. I felt every emotion there was to feel all at once.

"Hey Carter."